CHAYA ROSE:
A Mother's Love

Jacqueline Gutstein

CHAYA PUBLISHING

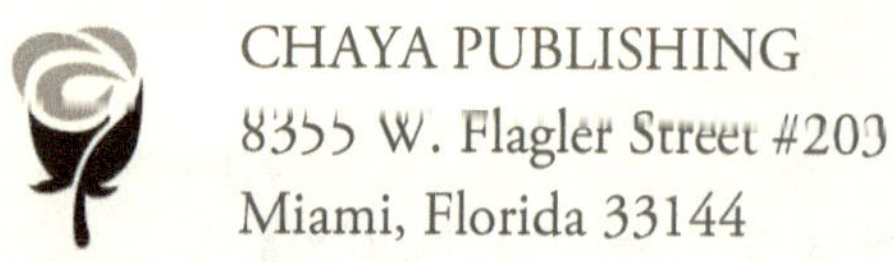

CHAYA PUBLISHING
8355 W. Flagler Street #203
Miami, Florida 33144

CHAYA PUBLISHING and colophon are
trademarks of CHAYA ROSE CORPORATION.

Published by: CHAYA PUBLISHING, Miami, Florida
Editor: Sharon Harvey Rosenberg

www.ChayaRoseBook.net
Inquiries: JacquelineGutstein@att.net, ChayaRose@att.net

Library of Congress Control Number: 2019901802

ISBN: 978-1-7337203-0-4

First Edition

Printed in the United States of America

10 9 8 7 6 5 4 3 2 1

DEDICATION

To all the birth Mothers

who gave the gift of life,

the families that adopted them,

and to the adopted children who

make this world a better place.

AUTHOR'S NOTE

When I set out to write this book, I wanted to bring awareness of adoption through a story of love and inspiration, and how we can change the world with kindness. Placing a baby for adoption is one of the most selfless acts a woman can do. There are many reasons a baby is placed for adoption; each one a personal tale. It is not a simple choice, and not a choice to be taken lightly, but that choice may give a child a chance for a better future, and that child, may be the one that changes the world.

I also wanted to help provide some answers to those who have been adopted and keep asking themselves what I call the four Ws; Who, What, When, and Why. Why did my birth mother and father place me up for adoption? What happened in my mother's life that made her choose adoption? When was I born? Who are my birth parents?

It is unfortunate that many adopted children may never receive answers to their questions and are left wondering, since many adoptees never find and create a relationship with their birth parents. Others are able to reunite with one or both of their birth parents with the help of online sites that specialize in reunifications and it changes their lives.

Doing research for this book, I read many moving stories about adoption. One thing I know for sure is that there are so many families who desperately want to bear a child, and for one reason or another cannot. It happened in my own immediate family, so I am aware of the pain those couples deal with.

As a family member and his wife were preparing for the birth of their first child, I wondered what this little baby that was still in the womb would be like, and what he may grow up to be one day. I couldn't wait to meet the little guy and wondered what talents he will possess that may change this world, and make it a better place. I wrote this poem and dedicated it to him, and to all the future souls that are yet to be born.

Uncovered

An artist is born with a blank canvas to paint

With their own imagination;

A singer is born with a song that has yet to be sung;

A poet is born with words and rhyme

Swirling in their minds;

A photographer is born with their own vision of the world;

A writer is born with thoughts that need to be expressed;

Every soul has its potential, yet to be uncovered,

Like a rose unfolding its petals.

The best is yet to come…

- Jacqueline Gutstein

ACKNOWLEDGMENTS

MY DEEP APPRECIATION GOES TO CHAYA "ROSA" KAMENSKY, my grandmother, and the inspiration for this book, whose spirit guided me throughout the process.

A special thank you to my editor, Sharon Harvey Rosenberg, for her insight, talent, and guidance. Her input was invaluable to the story. And my gratitude to Patte Beans who helped me fine-tune the very early drafts.

Finally, I want to give my sincere gratitude to the birth mothers and fathers around the world who chose to place their children for adoption, and those families who adopted and gave them a loving home. I will be forever grateful to all of you.

CONTENTS

1 | Memories Of My Childhood
By Rose Summer Stuart

I can't remember a time when a baby wasn't roaming the house. My momma, Chaya Rose, would be cradling a crying child, feeding a hungry one, changing a diaper, or just giving a shoulder and a loving ear to whomever needed to be listened to.

I thought I was the luckiest child in the world to have so many brothers and sisters. Sometimes it was chaotic, yet at the same time, it felt like a small orchestra that never skipped a beat, with Momma acting as the conductor. Every morning while I was fast asleep, she kissed my forehead, gently rocking my body until I awakened and whispered in my ears the same five words: "Wake up my little angel." I always found that amusing, because much of the time we were such a handful.

Hearing those words first thing every morning brought a strange comfort as I wriggled under the blankets and struggled to open my eyes.

A warm glass of milk was always on the night table waiting to greet me as I got up and sat on the edge of the bed, my feet dangling over the side as I rubbed my eyes with my knuckles. To this day, I stare at my night table when I wake up in the morning and I swear, for one split second, I can see a glass of milk there.

Momma was stern with us every now and then when she needed to be, but she took immense joy in allowing us just to be kids. Now looking back, it was as if she was living her life all over again through us. Having been raised an only child, Momma missed out on the interaction that a large family of rambunctious kids provides.

Whatever circumstances arose, her heart was always tender with us. She possessed an uncanny understanding of our every sorrow and our joys, rarely interfering with the spontaneous makings of what she knew would be future treasured childhood memories.

We lived in an old, two-story farmhouse in the rural countryside of Tennessee that had been in the family for several generations. Momma's great granddaddy, Parker T. Rose, built the farmhouse with his bare hands in the mid-1800s.

A carpenter by trade, he ran a small furniture and hardware store that supplied the town with much needed goods. People would make the journey from miles away to see Parker's custom-made furniture, each one a masterpiece in itself. In those days, the store brought him notoriety and a moderate income to sustain his family.

The farmhouse had five bedrooms, a modest kitchen, a small library with shelving that wrapped around the room from the ceiling to the floor, and an adjacent large living room specifically designed for entertaining. All the cabinets and furniture throughout the house were handmade by Parker with attention paid to functionality and the detail he had a reputation for.

The living room was immense and the hardwood floors were covered with a variety of area rugs that we used as magic carpets to slide around the house with. Although the room was designed for entertaining with its elegant tea tables and inviting sitting areas, the only entertaining our family did was to chase each other around during the day, and to read by the fireplace come nightfall. Folks just lived too far for visiting, and Momma had a very limited social life.

Every window of the house had a view of the large trees that encircled the grounds and offered shelter from the sun during the hot summer months. On a windy day, as the trees swayed with the elegance of a ballerina performing a dance, you could catch glimpses of the hills in the distance carpeted with green grass in the summer time. During the winter, the hills gleamed with white snow that seemed to go on endlessly, calling to be imprinted with our steps and homemade sleds that our family's longtime friend, Teddy, built for us.

The barn where the family furniture business began was situated behind the main house. Remnants of sawmills, wood planks, tree stumps and hundreds of tools lay untouched since Momma's father passed. Every afternoon after our home schooling, we transformed the barn into our playroom. We'd play hide and seek in the stacks of hay that were strewn along the back of barn adjacent to the old abandoned horse stables.

My brothers and sisters would climb a long wooden stepladder to the second level of the barn and we would jump down onto a huge pile of hay, always egging each other on to go one step higher and be more daring.

Even though I was terrified of heights, the day finally arrived when I got the courage to climb to the top step of the ladder. Shutting my eyes as tight as I could, I said a quick prayer and jumped while letting out a scream that could be heard from the main house. My brothers were so impressed that they never called me a sissy again, and I was bursting with joy at my accomplishment.

There was time to play and a time to help around the house, and there were plenty of chores to go around. As my brothers and sisters grew older, we were assigned different responsibilities depending on our age. We rotated chores so everyone had an opportunity to learn and experience all the jobs that needed to be done around the house and the grounds. The boys learned how to do the laundry, cook and clean, and the girls learned how to trim hedges, throw out the trash, unload hay and help with any light repairs. The younger children would pick up strewn toys lying around the house, while the older kids would either help with the housework, or help outdoors feeding our two cows that Momma named Hickory and Chicory.

My childhood memories always bring a smile to my face and a warm glow to my heart. The days were filled with the laughter of children and a sense of closeness and love.

Today, when I look at my own grandchildren playing in the yard, I think of the zebra swallowtail butterflies I chased into the fields with Momma. I think of Teddy, who was a dear friend of the family, and how he'd swoop me into the air and gave me a sense of security in his big strong arms, never complaining even when I picked and plucked endlessly at his kinky hair.

And I think of the sweet innocence that we grew up with, the tenderness of my mother, and the love she surrounded us with. I couldn't have asked for a better childhood. I hope I gave my family as much love as Momma gave us.

2 | Young Love

"For it was not into my ear you whispered, but into my heart. It was not my lips you kissed, but my soul."
~ Judy Garland

At the age of eighteen, Chaya's parents passed away and she inherited the farmhouse and a modest amount of savings from the family furniture business. It wasn't easy to live as a young, unmarried woman in rural Tennessee without any family nearby. Even though she loved to paint for fun as a young child, now it became her escape and a way to make the extra money she needed to support herself.

Chaya was brilliant at painting spectacular landscapes with flowing rivers and grassy rolling hills, pictures that invited the viewer to escape their own reality, and envision themselves surrounded by natural beauty and bliss. Her paintings drew rave reviews and were featured in numerous art galleries throughout Tennessee.

Although Chaya never married, she was in love once with a neighboring boy named Michael. They were in their young teens when they met at the annual county fair and he was instantly smitten with her looks and her infectious laugh. It was love at first sight as he saw her sipping cold ice tea near the food stand. Chaya was a beautiful, tall young girl with reddish brown curly hair that caressed her shoulders. Her porcelain complexion was smooth as silk to the touch, and she possessed dazzling azure blue eyes.

Michael, a year older than Chaya, was tall and handsome. His eyes were caramel brown framed by long thick eyelashes, and his dark straight brown hair was trimmed short and parted slightly off center. Michael's full red lips were well defined, and he had a small dimple on his chin that Chaya found attractive.

Michael constantly reminded her she could make him act like a fumbling child whenever she was around. He would pick colorful flowers for Chaya from his family's garden, and compose romantic poems which he would recite with the drama of an actor in a play. It wasn't long before he swept her off her feet with his courting rituals, and she fell hopelessly in love with him.

But Chaya's father didn't approve of how much time they were spending together after school and on weekends. Often gone for hours, the young couple picnicked by the lake bordering the well-known Williams family ranch a few miles away. The lake was covered with water lilies and an endless array of wildlife that provided entertainment with their mating rituals. Chaya and Michael felt a strong spiritual connection with each other, and being at this lake provided them the serenity and privacy they longed for.

After a two-year courtship, Michael worked up the courage and asked Chaya to be his wife one afternoon as they sat lakeside. He meticulously prepared a picnic basket with two sandwiches, a bottle of wine he 'borrowed' from his father's liquor cabinet, and two drinking cups. Underneath the cloth napkins he carefully folded on top of the blanket he lay on the ground, Michael placed a small velvet box for her to find.

After reaching for the napkin to place on her lap, Chaya found the box and excitedly clutched it to her chest.

Chaya held her breath while she slowly opened the box, her jaw opening wide as she slowly pulled out the ring. Michael excitably reached over to hold the ring, and placed it on the third finger of her trembling right hand while he got on one knee and proposed to her. It was the most beautiful ring she had ever seen and Chaya enthusiastically accepted the proposal while she flung her arms around him. Michael's grandmother had left the heirloom to her eldest grandson hoping one day he would find the perfect woman to marry and to wear her ring.

But before they could marry, Michael wanted to get permission from Chaya's father, Mr. Rose, because of their young age, and because it was the honorable thing to do. Michael chose the day carefully, knowing that Chaya's father would be home, relaxing in his favorite rocking chair. Too nervous to eat breakfast, Michael dressed up in the only Sunday suit he owned. It had been well over a year since the last time he'd worn it, and it looked to be a couple of sizes too small. To make a good impression, Michael chose his favorite white shirt that needed a bit more ironing, and borrowed his father's dark blue tie.

How he wished he had paid more attention to his father's instruction when he tried to teach him to make a proper tie knot years earlier. After what seemed like an eternity in front of his bedroom mirror, Michael finally mastered a knot that was presentable.

Today was the day he would ask Chaya's father if he could have his daughter's hand in marriage. Even though Michael had just turned seventeen, he was confident he would make a good husband and would do whatever it took to care and provide for his beautiful Chaya.

Mr. Rose, Chaya's father, was a commanding figure, demanding respect, and Michael always referred to him in a proper manner, calling him Mr. Rose and sir when in his presence.

Although the respect Michael had for him bordered on terror at times, today he felt confident to look Mr. Rose in the eyes and ask for his daughter's hand in marriage. Michael loved Chaya deeply and he knew she was the one he wanted to spend the rest of his life with. They didn't want to be apart any longer, and being married would allow them to be together every day and possibly start a family sooner, rather than later.

Michael took one long deep breath, swallowing hard as he slowly walked up what seemed to be an endless amount of porch steps at the Rose house. With each step he took, the wooden planks creaked louder and louder, and when Michael finally reached the front door, his mind raced with thoughts about how he would begin the most important conversation of his life.

He anticipated Mrs. Rose would open the door like she normally did, but to his dismay, Mr. Rose swung the door wide open, holding it back with a stiff outstretched arm. Michael could feel his white shirt cling to his sweat-lined body. He could see his chest heaving in and out in a desperate attempt to catch his breath. Caught a little by surprise that Michael was dressed so formal, Mr. Rose stood stoically silent and stared at him, still holding the door wide open.

Within seconds, Mrs. Rose joined her husband at the door and welcomed Michael in from the heat of the day. She offered him some cold iced tea, and he immediately gulped the entire glass without taking a breath. A little aghast at the hastiness in which Michael drank the tea, Mrs. Rose offered him another serving, but he politely declined and cleared his throat several times.

"If I may, Mr. Rose, could I have a word with you alone?" Michael asked, while looking apologetically at Mrs. Rose for not inviting her to stay for the conversation.

The Roses stared at each other for a moment, and Mrs. Rose graciously excused herself and quietly disappeared into the kitchen while Mr. Rose sat down in his favorite rocking chair.

Michael took one last deep breath before he went straight to point of his visit.

"Mr. Rose, I've known your daughter for a long time now. You've done a wonderful job raising Chaya, and sir, I love her with all my heart and she loves me."

Mr. Rose stared at Michael with a stoic face already anticipating where this conversation was heading, but letting him finish his prepared speech.

"What I'm trying to say, sir, is that I am here to respectfully ask for her hand in marriage. I promise to take good care of her and to protect and provide for her the rest of our lives just like you and Mrs. Rose."

Before Michael could utter another word, Mr. Rose replied with his stern voice. "Too young!" he said abruptly while slapping the arms of his chair with his palms. "What's the rush young man? You think you have this all figured out don't you? Well, this is not going to happen! Never!"

Michael was taken aback, but he pleaded with Mr. Rose to give him a chance and reminded him again how dedicated he was to Chaya and that he would not let him down. But Mr. Rose had other plans for his only daughter. He wanted her to go to college and make something of herself. Maybe become a doctor or a lawyer or even president of the United States someday, and Michael would only hold her back. He believed marriage was difficult enough, and he deemed them too naive and too young for a lifelong commitment.

His answer was simply a resounding, "No!"

Michael was devastated. He had known there was a chance Mr. Rose would be hesitant, but he hadn't prepared for total rejection, and he knew Chaya would be distraught when she heard her father's reply.

Michael planned to meet Chaya by the lake with the good news, but instead found himself frozen, unable to move after he stumbled out of the Rose home and slowly climbed down the creaky steps. After what seemed like an eternity staring at the ground, he began walking towards the lake where Chaya was waiting for him with all the hopes and dreams of young love. It was a while before he realized he hadn't taken off his suit jacket or even loosened his knotted tie. Now it seemed to be choking him.

By the time he reached the lake, his body was drenched with perspiration from the mid-day sun and his face was beet red with dozens of water droplets forming above his upper lip. His perfectly coiffed hair now fell recklessly around his face and with his head hanging low, he gingerly approached Chaya and stood in front of her.

Without Michael uttering a single word, Chaya came to the apparent conclusion that the conversation between Michael and her father didn't go so well.

"I can't believe this!" shouted Chaya in disbelief. "My father is wrong. I love you, Michael, with all my heart and there's no one, not even my father that is going to ever change that."

"I love you too, Chaya," Michael uttered as he reached for her hands.

Michael brought her in close to him until her body touched his, and they held each other tighter than they ever had as tears streamed down both their faces. As Michael began to wipe away the tears on her ruddy cheeks with the back of his hand, Chaya took his hand in hers. They wanted to not only be able to be in each other's arms every day, but every night as well and be able share their love, emotionally and physically. Their young strong bodies ached with the longing to make love to one another.

"Let's get married!" Chaya blurted out. "Right here Michael. Right now. Let's say the vows we had planned on saying and let God marry us."

"You're serious about this Chaya?"

"I've never been more serious in my life."

Michael and Chaya took a step back from each other and held each other's hands and as Michael was about to utter his vows, he looked into Chaya's loving blue eyes as if he was looking at her for the first time, totally mesmerized. Although he'd never seen the ocean in person, he could imagine what color it must look like just by looking into her eyes. With wild butterflies fluttering in circles around them and the crisp blue sky as their witness, they recited their vows to each other.

Michael began, "I, Michael, want to spend the rest of my life together with you, Chaya, to have and to hold, from this day on. I will cherish you, and honor you as a friend, a lover and faithful husband. I will be by your side in sickness and in health, until death do us part."

Chaya's eyes welled up with tears. Michael was the man of her dreams, and she was about to marry him.

"I, Chaya Rose, want to spend the rest of my life together with you, Michael, to have and to hold, from this day on. I will cherish you, and honor you as a friend, a lover and faithful wife. I will be by your side in sickness and in health, until death do us part. May our souls become one on this day under the eyes of God. Amen."

"Amen."

Chaya and Michael wept with joy as they embraced and sealed the marriage with the most passionate kiss they'd ever given one another. Today was the day they would become one, both emotionally and physically. Their bodies gently fell to the ground, beside the lake where they spent endless hours together, and made love for the first time. In their hearts, their marriage and the bond they shared would never be broken. Today would be the beginning of their new life.

Chaya and Michael promised each other not to tell a soul about their union. Determined not to argue with her father on this special day in her life, Chaya adjusted her clothing, fixed her hair, and acted as though nothing happened as she walked back towards her house. When she arrived home late that afternoon, her father was rocking back and forth in his chair at a quick pace, waiting for her.

"Hi Daddy!" she beamed working hard to keep her composure as she walked into the house.

She adored and admired her father, but she was not willing to give up Michael either. In their hearts they were married now under the eyes of God, and she was determined to keep it a secret.

Mr. Rose was taken aback by her nonchalant demeanor and wasn't sure if his daughter knew Michael had visited him hours before asking for her hand in marriage. He continued to study her expression in a futile attempt to figure out if she knew Michael's intentions.

"Where have you been, Chaya?" he questioned her with an unusually serious expression. "You've been gone for quite some time."

"Oh Daddy, it was such a beautiful day, I decided to go for a walk," she answered casually seeming not to have a care in the world. "Where's mother?"

"Uh, I think she's upstairs," he answered bewildered.

He was sure Michael would have told her he didn't approve of their marriage, but what if she didn't know anything? Would telling her Michael's intentions throw her into his arms even more?

Many thoughts raced through his head. If he demanded her not to see Michael ever again, he would have to explain why. He thought it best to see how things played out, because Mr. Rose loved his daughter dearly and the last thing he wanted was to cause a rift between them.

Mr. Rose was a towering figure, who despite having had a very sickly childhood, made a decent living building handmade custom wood furniture just like his father and grandfather did.

His hands were strong and calloused, but when it came to his little girl, his heart was compassionate.

As weeks passed, Chaya and Michael took advantage of every opportunity to see each other at the lake and more often than not, they ended up making love. He made sure to be cautious in order not to disgrace his new "bride" and they looked forward to the day when they would be old enough to officially marry and make a loving home together.

3 | Growing Up

*"It takes courage to grow up and become who you
really are." ~ E. E. Cummings*

The day began as any other summer morning. The sky
was clear with barely a cloud in sight, and the sun's rays were
beaming down. Chaya showered and came downstairs for her
favorite breakfast which included fresh baked sourdough bread,
buttermilk hotcakes, strawberries and eggs fried sunny-side up.

It was Sunday, and the family always ate breakfast
together. "Have any plans today, sweetheart?" her mother asked
while warming up the maple syrup on the stove.

"Oh it's such a beautiful day, I think I'm going to visit the
orphanage and take some of the kids outside to play in the
park," responded Chaya with elation in her voice. "I really enjoy
being with them."

"How long will you be volunteering there young lady?"

"Up until school starts again. The kids just love it when I
spend time with them and I guess they don't have too many
visitors."

Mr. Rose was extremely proud his daughter was spending
time at the orphanage. If someone like her had visited him when

he was growing up in the home for boys, it would have made it all the more bearable. Instead, Mr. Rose grew up alone, scared, and without an identity since no one knew his birth parents, or his name when he was dropped off at the orphanage by a young girl in her mid-teens. The staff at the home decided to name him Richard, after the doctor that first examined him when he arrived.

The other boys would tease him about his tall height and his thin awkward limbs, calling him nicknames like string bean and shoelace. Richard wasn't the fighting kind, so even though he was the tallest kid in the orphanage, he could never bring himself to hit another boy. His life changed when he turned thirteen and came to live with the Rose family.

The Roses' had been happily married for over fifteen years and although Jonathon T. Rose Sr. had two beautiful daughters, he longed for a son to pass on the family name. He and his wife, Victoria, who was now past child bearing age, spoke to an agency about adopting a young boy.

When Jonathon Sr. visited the home for boys, Richard, the sad gangly boy who rarely made eye contact caught his attention. There was something special about him that stood out among the rest. Richard had a simplicity about him that Jonathon Sr. related to almost immediately. That very day, he brought the boy home to live with them and shortly afterwards, Richard officially became Jonathon Richard Rose, Jr.

Like his adoptive father, Jonathon Jr. also dreamt of having his own family one day. Now, with his lovely wife and beautiful daughter, Chaya, he couldn't have been happier. He was a good husband and he was determined to be a good father to his daughter, promising himself that his child would never go without love like he did for so many years.

After breakfast, Chaya began her one-hour walk towards the orphanage. It was an unusually hot morning and the sun's rays were beating down on her like shards of hot metal. Chaya started to perspire profusely and her forehead was instantly covered in beads of sweat. Suddenly, she felt queasy and very weak.

"What's wrong with me?" she asked herself.

The sky began to swirl as she dropped to her knees and the breakfast she ate a short time earlier was stirring in her stomach. On the ground in the middle of the dirt road she was walking along, Chaya sprung out on all four limbs and with her back arched, took one deep breath and vomited.

She felt very weak and nauseous, but managed to stand up and head back home, her hands and knees covered with dirt. Chaya's white-laced blouse was drenched with perspiration and clung tightly to her slim figure. A few weeks ago, her mother had been ill with a stomach ailment, so Chaya assumed she'd caught the same bug.

"The children will be so disappointed," she mumbled to herself. "I'll make it up to them next week."

In the following days, Chaya struggled to keep down any solid food and she began to lose weight. Michael was very worried and he visited every day, even though Mr. Rose always made him feel uneasy. Although Chaya insisted she had developed a stomach bug, Mrs. Rose decided it was time to take her daughter to the doctor, fearing something was terribly wrong.

The doctor's visit was a short one.

Chaya was pregnant.

The car ride back home was an uncomfortable one. Her mother was in tears and she could barely utter a word.

"How could this happen?" was all she could muster to say over and over to herself, shaking her head in disbelief.

Chaya sat motionless, and in a barely audible voice, she said, "I'm so sorry, mother. I'm so sorry."

"You're going to kill your father with this, Chaya. You know he has a weak heart. He won't let you keep this baby. It'll ruin your reputation and our reputation. You know how small this town is. I'm sorry too, but you just can't keep this baby. How in the world am I going to tell your father?"

As soon as they arrived home, Chaya ran up the stairs to her room in tears without as much as a hello to her father. Mr. Rose, who was sick with worry, watched his daughter hurriedly pass right by him.

"What in the world is going on, Martha?"

"I'm afraid you'd better sit down, honey. It's Chaya. I don't know how else to tell you than just to tell you."

"Tell me what? What?"

"Chaya is pregnant."

"That Michael boy!" fumed Mr. Rose with his arms flailing in the air as he paced endlessly around the room in no particular direction.

"I'm going to kill him!"

"I knew he was trouble the minute I laid my eyes on him. And my little girl. How could my little girl do this to me, and to us? What did we do wrong Martha? I thought we raised her to know what's right and what's wrong, damn it. She's not keeping it. That's final!

Upstairs in her room, Chaya heard her father's rant. She was emotionally devastated and the disappointment in her father's voice was almost too much to bear. Chaya couldn't stand the thought of how much hurt she caused him.

Mr. Rose stormed out of the house not knowing exactly where he was headed. All he knew was that his heart was just broken and as much as he wanted to go and hold Chaya and let her know he would take care of things, he could not bear to look at her right now, and he wondered if he ever would.

Mrs. Rose went upstairs to check on Chaya and found her daughter sitting on the floor in the back corner of her bedroom with her arms wrapped around her legs, rocking herself back and forth.

"Oh Momma, what have I done?" she asked in desperation.

"Chaya, we can't turn back the clock, but we can try to put this behind us."

"I don't want to give up my baby," she wailed through her tears. "I know I'm young, but I'll take good care of my child. Don't make me do that! I'll do anything, but don't make me do that."

Mrs. Rose was so torn. She knew the reason that her husband was here today was because his mother made the decision to send her son to an orphanage where he was finally adopted, but he also grew up without a family for many years. And now she was telling her child to give away her own baby.

"Chaya, you can't keep this child," pleaded Mrs. Rose. "Your father won't permit it. It would bring shame on this family."

"Mother, I want to keep my baby so much, but if Daddy won't permit it, then I'll leave for a couple of months when I start showing and have the baby in another town," Chaya said, finally relenting.

"No one will know. If I have to give up my child, at least let me give it a chance at having a life with loving parents. Can you help me find a good family that will take care of my baby?"

"Of course we will. Your father and I will make sure of it."

4 | Goodbyes

"Children and mothers never truly part, bound together by the beating of one another's heart" ~ Charlotte Gray

Chaya's parents found a home for mothers-to-be who were planning on placing their babies for adoption over 40 miles away in a small town outside of Tennessee. Chaya left early that winter when she started showing a belly.

She left without saying a word to Michael, knowing it would be too difficult not to tell him if she said her goodbyes. The labor was difficult, but after thirty long agonizing hours, Chaya gave birth to a beautiful and healthy baby girl. Although she managed to get a quick glimpse of the baby, she never got a chance to hold her before the nurses whisked her away to another room.

Chaya named her baby girl Summer Michael Rose.

Michael never knew why Chaya had left town so abruptly without saying a word to him and he was truly concerned, not only for her health, but her safety. Chaya's parents only told him that their daughter needed to get some special treatment for her stomach ailment and had to leave to go to a medical clinic far away until she recuperated.

When Chaya returned back home after the birth of her daughter, she mostly kept to herself and would rarely venture out of her home. After Michael heard she was back in town, he wrote her letters and poems, and dropped them off in her mailbox hoping she would reach out to him. When school finished for the day, he took a longer way home just so he could walk pass Chaya's house hoping to get a glimpse of her outside, but to no avail.

Michael passed by her house regularly and asked for her, but each time, Chaya refused to meet or speak with him. Every time she heard his voice at the front door, a flood of emotions would overcome her and she struggled not to call out and embrace him.

Since Chaya didn't tell Michael of the pregnancy, she alone had to live with the fact she'd placed the baby that they created on their "wedding" day for adoption. The very thought of Michael reminded her of the little baby girl who would never know her parents and never know how much she was loved.

Chaya knew how much Michael wanted to start a family one day, so she truly believed not knowing his child's whereabouts would drive him insane. Anyways, it was too late to tell him now and she prayed the Lord would forgive her for that one day.

After months of attempting to reach Chaya, Michael eventually resigned himself to the fact that their relationship was over, but he didn't understand why, and he never ever stopped loving her. Meanwhile, the guilt of her secret was overwhelming Chaya and it took a toll on her spirit and zest for life. Chaya's relationship with her father was never quite the same again and there was only silence now, when chatter usually permeated their Sunday breakfast. She only spoke when spoken to and her responses were concise and void of any outward emotion.

Chaya's heart was broken and the memory of her baby's wailing during the delivery rang in her ears like the echo of a constantly ringing bell. In the evening, when the wind blew against her bedroom window panes, it made a whistling sound, mimicking a baby's cry. Believing this cry was her baby calling out to her, she covered her ears and hummed to drown out the noise.

As Mother's Day approached, the pain of not having her baby girl with her became unbearable. Knowing this day would be particularly difficult for her daughter, Chaya's mother asked her to take a walk with her after breakfast and to bring a pad or writing paper and a pencil. They walked to the same lake where Chaya and Michael spent their days and sat down on a blanket that Mrs. Rose had brought along with her.

"Chaya, I want you to do something for me on this Mother's Day," her mother began to say. "It's really for you and to begin the healing process. I know you miss your daughter tremendously, so why don't you write a letter to her and let her know how much you love and miss her? I used to do this when my mother passed away and it helped me connect with her in some way."

"Mom, I want my daughter back with me where she belongs," Chaya cried out. "I never even got a chance to hold her."

"Chaya, your daughter is going to grow up with a loving family who couldn't have another baby of their own. She's going to be happy and I'm sure she'll grow up to be a wonderful young lady."

Chaya wiped the tears from her cheeks and grabbed hold of the pad of paper and pencil and began to write a letter to her little baby as her mother suggested. As she started to write, a flood of emotion came over her and she tried desperately to capture her emotions on paper.

It was important to Chaya that her baby, Summer Michael Rose, never doubt her birth mother's love. She had an overwhelming need to make sure her daughter never felt abandoned as her own father had felt. Her daughter deserved to know the 'whys' in her life and writing the letter would allow her to be the one to tell her.

5 | The First Letter
Mother's Day 1947

"Eloquent speech is not from lip to ear, but rather from heart to heart." ~ William Jennings

Dear Summer,

This is my first Mother's Day letter to you. My heart is torn with both sorrow and joy. I wish I could have held you if only for one second. I never got the chance, my little angel. Oh, and you did look like an angel. You had beautiful pink skin and your tiny mouth was stretched open so wide when the doctors delivered you into this world. Chances are you're probably going to be a singer with those strong pair of lungs you have.

Your hair was matted wet and clung to your small head swirling in different directions. Someday it'll be long enough to comb into little pigtails and tie with pink ribbons. I can picture you as a young lady in a little white dress, with ruffles and lace trim.

You gave me a little struggle there, young lady. I thought you were never going to arrive, and I didn't blame you because this world isn't always easy to live in. But I cherished every moment I carried you inside of me and I know Michael would have been so proud.

Yes, Summer, Michael is your daddy. He's so handsome, spontaneous, thoughtful, and generous, and I hope you inherited these wonderful traits from him. He would have been there for you if he knew you were coming into this world. I pray that you will forgive me for not telling him about you. You see, an unmarried young girl just can't tarnish the family name with a child out of wedlock and my father didn't allow me to keep you.

I wanted to give you a chance at life and hope for your future, so I decided placing you for adoption with a loving family was the best thing for you. It was so gut-wrenching to feel you growing in my tummy, feeling your kicks and restlessness, and then hearing your cries, knowing that strangers would be taking you away from me when you were born. The staff at the hospital and social services told me you were placed with a wonderful and caring family who will take care of you. Please know that you will always have my soul within you no matter where you are or what is going on in your life. That mother-daughter bond will never be taken away from us.

My precious Summer, you were truly a gift from God. I will always pray for you and be with you. When you are scared…when you are happy…and whenever you need a hug, wrap your arms around yourself, close your eyes, and picture a beautiful blooming rose, with dozens of petals enveloping you with love. That'll be me. I'll be right there hugging you back. Always.

I love you my sweet angel. More than you'll ever know. I will always love you and I pray to the good Lord every day to take good care of you and to allow me to meet you one day and to hold you in my arms. Until then, goodbye my dear Summer.

I love you so much,
Mommy

Although it was difficult to write the letter, Chaya found that writing to Summer gave her the opportunity to express her deepest emotions to her daughter, and over the next several weeks and months, she began the healing process and was already looking forward to writing the next letter.

Every year on Mother's Day, Chaya wrote a letter to Summer hoping that one day, she would be able to give the letters she wrote to her daughter, and to let her know she was loved every day of her life. It was in the writing of the letters that Chaya took comfort and found her strength again.

She started looking forward to Mother's Day for there were dozens of thoughts and dreams she wanted to convey to her baby girl. She wanted to play some part in the priceless moments Summer would be going through in the future like her first steps, her first baby tooth, and her first day at school, even though she would be unable to witness them herself.

Chaya needed to convey to Summer that she was not alone in the world and that her mother would always be right there by her side, praying for her, and loving her, but most of all, wishing she could be there with her. Chaya stored the letters she wrote in a box she made with the wood and tools stored in their farmhouse barn. She carved Summer's full name and a rose on the lid of the box and stored it safely in the night table next to her bed.

Chaya never finished high school and never returned to visit the orphanage where she volunteered, because it was just too difficult for her. She kept to herself, painting the beautiful landscapes around her property, and rarely left the house that was once filled with joy and laughter.

Mr. Rose passed away two years later of a sudden heart attack while he was shoveling snow to clear the driveway and it was a devastating blow to Chaya and her mother. Even though their relationship had been strained since the baby's birth, Chaya adored her father since he had always been there for her growing up. She never forgave him for forcing her to give up her child, but Chaya made peace with it and at least her daughter had a chance to grow up.

Less than six months later, Chaya lost her dear mother as she passed quietly in her sleep. The doctor told Chaya her mother died of natural causes, but Chaya believed she died of a broken heart. Mr. Rose was everything to her mother and they were very close soulmates who could finish each other's sentences without skipping a beat. With both her parents gone, Chaya felt more alone than she'd ever felt in her life.

6 | A Knock On The Door

"Be not forgetful to entertain strangers for thereby
some have entertained angels unawares. "
~ Hebrews 13:2

The persistent knock on the door startled Chaya since she wasn't used to visitors. The closest neighbor was miles away, and she rarely left her home anymore except to place her paintings in the art galleries and stores on consignment. As Chaya opened the door wide enough to peer through the opening, she saw a young girl that looked to be in her teens, twirling her long black hair nervously with both hands.

"Can I help you young lady?" asked Chaya cautiously.

"I'm sorry to bother you ma'am, but Pastor John gave me your name," said the teen.

"He said you were great with children and that you had this big house all to yourself and that you might be able to help me."

"I don't understand, miss," Chaya responded not knowing what else to say.

"How can I possibly help you?"

"I'm not from here," the girl said, her voice now

trembling. "You see, my parents told me I couldn't keep my baby, and if I did, I would have to leave the house for good."

Chaya stood there, shocked at what she was hearing.

"I need a place to stay until I deliver my baby and find a good home for it. I'm only sixteen…I can't keep this child. The Pastor said you had five bedrooms and were alone, and might be up to some company. I have some money my parents gave me and some that I earned doing odd jobs. I'm starting to show a belly, so my parents threw me out of the house and told me I could only come back if I come back without the baby. They said I was an embarrassment to them. I can give you that money to help with expenses."

Chaya hadn't even noticed the girl was pregnant since she was wearing a loose fitting blouse.

"I don't know why this Pastor John gave you my name," said Chaya who was visibly upset and fighting back tears.

"I haven't been to church in years. How could he send you to me? What was he thinking?"

"I'm so sorry," the young girl said. "It was a mistake to come here. I just didn't know where else to go. Obviously, the Pastor who gave me your name was mistaken. Again, I'm so sorry."

As the young girl turned to go, Chaya shouted out to her.

"No, wait!" Chaya said grabbing the girl's arm to prevent her from leaving.

"I don't know a Pastor John or why he sent you to me, but I know how you must feel. I do have the room, and I could use the company. I'm not exactly sure why, but maybe you were sent here for a reason. I think it's about time I started living again."

"Forgive me. Where are my manners? Please, come in. I don't even know your name."

The girl picked up the small suitcase she brought along and Chaya led her into the house, closing the door behind them.

"My name is Heather. Heather Stuart and I'm pregnant, scared and I feel so alone. Even my boyfriend left me after he found out he was going to be a father. He said he wasn't ready for all that responsibility and he wanted to finish high school."

Suddenly, Chaya saw a younger version of herself only four years earlier. She was the same age as Heather when she became pregnant and she too, was scared and felt all alone. Chaya remembered being told by her own parents that she couldn't stay and have her baby. The similarities were uncanny.

Chaya invited Heather to sit down in the living room and gave her a glass of water. All the emotions she felt as a sixteen year old pregnant teenager began coming back, but this time she somehow felt different. Instead of feeling sad, she looked forward to seeing this new life that would be arriving in the coming months.

"Tell me something Heather," Chaya was wondering. "Do you love this baby you are carrying?

"I love this baby more than anything in the world and I want this child to have a future with a good family," Heather said.

Have you thought of what it means to give up your child?" Chaya asked wanting to make sure Heather had thought this through carefully.

"Jimmy and I loved each other when we created this baby, but we're both sixteen and as I said, he's not ready to be a father. I have nothing to give this baby."

"Oh, but you do have something to give this child," Chaya responded, tightly holding Heather's hands. "You have a gift that is priceless. It's precious, it's free and it's never ending.

You have the gift of a mother's love and don't you ever forget that young lady. I'll tell you what, I'll let you stay here under one condition."

Heather listened anxiously not knowing what would be the condition she would have to fulfill.

"You must promise to write a letter to your baby every year on Mother's Day until your child becomes an adult. You could begin by describing what your childhood and family life were like. You could tell your child about Jimmy, the boy you fell in love with who became the birth father. Tell your child how scared and alone you felt, and that you had to leave your home in order to give birth." Heather was listening intently to every word Chaya was saying.

"In other words, describe your journey. How you ended up here at my home and what it felt like when the baby was kicking up a storm in your belly. Describe what the birth was like. Your child will want to know all the details. And especially answer the 'whys' that this child is sure to ask later in life."

"Explain why you decided to place your baby for adoption, how you felt about this, and what your hopes and dreams are for your baby. This will be very important to your child as he or she grows older. You can also write about your joys, your thoughts and your worries. I want you to send me the letters every year and I will keep them for your baby, and one day, when the time is right, I will make sure your child receives them wherever he or she may be. Promise me this, and I will let you stay. You don't have to pay me absolutely anything."

Tears streamed down Heather's face, as she was certain she had made the right choice. Heather promised to write the letters, without hesitation. "Thank you, thank you so much. I don't know how I'll ever repay you."

7 | A New Beginning

*"I have a crystal-clear understanding about my purpose
in life, which I didn't before, and it's to love her all the days
I'm allowed to." - Hoda Koth, on becoming an
adoptive mother to Haley Joy*

The birth came sooner than expected. After nine hours of labor, Chaya and a local mid-wife delivered a beautiful baby girl Heather named Rose, in honor of the woman who opened up her home and her heart to her. The home birth went smoothly and without any complications.

Chaya gently took the baby girl from the mid-wife and placed her in Heather's arms, encouraging her to hold the baby for as long as she wanted. It was something she never got a chance to do herself and regretted to this day. No mother should be denied a chance to hold her own baby, and she knew all too well, the longing never goes away.

Chaya was so proud of Heather and her choice to give this baby a chance to grow up with a family that could take care of her. She could feel the love Heather had for her baby by the way she gently kissed the newborn's forehead over and over. Heather rubbed her own cheek, now moist with tears, against the baby's cheek to feel her skin and to smell her.

For the next several hours, Heather sat in Mr. Rose's old rocking chair Chaya prepared for her in the bedroom, gently caressing baby Rose in her arms, who was wrapped in a quilt that Chaya's mother made when Chaya was born. Heather sang the only lullabies she could remember the words to, whispering in her baby's ear, and sporadically planting kisses all over Rose's forehead, cheeks and belly.

Chaya quietly closed the door to their room giving them privacy, but left a small opening in case Heather needed her. Every so often Chaya would gingerly walk by and catch a glimpse of the new mother and baby. She knew these were precious moments that Heather would remember for the rest of her life.

It wasn't planned, but Heather asked Chaya if she would raise the baby instead of giving her to an adoption agency as they had previously agreed. She believed Chaya would be great with children and, after all, she had to have a big heart to allow a total stranger who was pregnant, to move into her home.

Chaya was overwhelmed Heather would entrust her with her baby. Before she could actually think of what it would entail, she agreed. Against Chaya's insistence, Heather moved out three days later and headed back home on a Greyhound bus. Chaya believed it was too soon for her to be traveling, but Heather was firm and insisted she needed to start putting her life back together again and the longer she stayed, the harder it would be.

Heather, still holding the baby, gave Chaya a tearful goodbye and thanked her for all she had done. She handed little Rose to Chaya, and as she turned to leave, gave the baby one last kiss on her forehead, and told her she would always be loved.

Finally, Chaya had a baby girl all to herself and she decided to add Summer as her middle name…Rose Summer Stuart. Rose was a beautiful baby with black hair, long fingers and fair skin. For Chaya, the baby's every smile, every giggle, and every cry was treasured.

Since she hadn't planned on raising the baby, Chaya enlisted the help of Teddy and together, they quickly built a wooden crib that Chaya could use to rock Rose back and forth.

The first of the letters from Heather came shortly after Mother's Day. She wrote two letters, one for Rose and one for Chaya. In the letter, Heather asked Chaya to keep her informed on how Rose was doing. She knew Chaya would be a great mother and that her daughter would be happy there, and she knew that one day, Rose would be given the letters she had written and know how much her birth mother loved her.

8 | Mother's Day 1950

"However motherhood comes to you, it's a miracle."
~ Valerie Harper

Dear Summer,

I was blessed this year with another daughter I named Rose Summer Stuart. You have a sister now, Summer. Rose is a miracle to me and her birth mother, Heather, was the same age as me when I delivered you.

She too wasn't allowed to keep her baby and stay at her parent's house like me, but she didn't have a place to go, so a Pastor she met sent her to me. I have no idea why, but I truly believe it was the good Lord's will.

Rose is so full of energy and such a happy baby. She's keeping me really busy and I hope I am being a good mother to her. Summer, I hope your parents are being good to you too.

I ache inside because you are not here with me. I spend an endless amount of time picturing what you look like now. Do you look like me, or do you look like your birth father Michael? Are you happy and healthy and do you feel loved? If I could turn back the clock, I would have never let you go, but I was so young and I was told it would be best for you.

Over the years, I have finally forgiven my parents for telling me I couldn't keep you. These letters that I write to you are helping me to heal and to continue the bond that I will forever have with you. I have to have faith that things in life happen for a reason, and you are better off with your new family.

I miss you terribly,
Your Mommy

9 | One Step At A Time

"The first steps a child takes are into your heart."
- Author unknown

One evening as Chaya was preparing supper, Rose stood in her wooden playpen with her small hands firmly grasping its rim. She turned around and took two wobbly steps towards her mother who was standing a couple of feet away before she fell on her behind with a thud.

Rose almost looked more surprised than Chaya at the feat she just accomplished. She mimicked the expression of joy on Chaya's face and let out bursts of continuous giggles.

"You did it Rosie!" Chaya shrieked with total elation as she leaned over into the playpen and scooped her daughter up in the air, twirling her round and round just like her own father did when Chaya was a baby. "You did it!"

Thoughts of Summer instantly raced through Chaya's mind like a car careening out of control. If only she could have seen Summer take her first steps, wobbling like someone trying to cross an old wooden canopy bridge suspended by ropes. Her tears of laughter eventually turned to tears of sorrow. Chaya knew there would be moments like this the rest of her life, because for every joyous accomplishment Rose did, Chaya imagined the moment in her mind with Summer. But Rose gave Chaya a new purpose in life, and Chaya gave Rose the kind of love only a mother could give a child.

A couple of weeks later, Rose began making her way alone from the jade-colored sofa in the main room to the antique cherry coffee table that Chaya's great, great grandfather made. Chaya would trail quietly just a few feet behind her so Rose would feel free to roam and explore. Eventually Rose would stop and turn around seeking the comfort of her mother, for somehow, she always knew she was not alone.

Chaya spent hours teaching her the names of different farm animals, and they enjoyed following the butterflies into the fields. The butterflies provided Rose something to walk towards, eventually enticing her to run in order to keep up with them.

Rose was fascinated by Teddy, a dear family friend and Chaya's confident, who came around once or twice a week to check up on them, keep the grounds groomed, and fix whatever needed fixing. He collected the money Chaya made from her oil paintings that sold in the galleries and stores around town, never accepting a dime for all his trouble.

Teddy was a fairly hefty, tall, dark-skinned man with big deep-set brown eyes and an afro that was beginning to turn gray. He always wore his traditional faded blue jean overalls with a white tee shirt that always appeared to be in need of a good bleaching. Protruding out of his back right pocket would be his signature red bandana, one of many he owned. Teddy used this bandana to wipe the sweat off his brow and around his thick neck, slowly stretching it upwards to collect the pools of sweat in between the folds of skin.

Teddy had known the Rose family for over thirty years, and promised Chaya's parents he would look after her if they ever passed on. He was a handyman in town, so he was free to come and go at his leisure.

Over the years, Chaya developed a deep fondness for Teddy, and came to depend on his visits for company and advice. He was a proud man with a gentle soul and both Chaya and Rose adored him. Although Teddy's wife died seventeen years before, he never remarried out of respect for her. They didn't have any children, so the time he spent with Chaya and Rose was precious to him.

Teddy's real name was Clarence, but Rose would have none of that. To her, he looked just like the brown teddy bear she hugged each night before going to sleep since both the bear and Clarence wore overalls.

Rose constantly tried to pull his kinky gray hairs straight in order to uncurl them, thinking they were snowflakes. Playing along with her, Teddy would ooh and aah when she tugged at them. He grabbed her little fingers before she could pull them away and this made Rose giggle and blush. She looked forward to his visits, and as soon as she heard his pickup truck in the distance, Rose would run down the front steps as fast as she could and jump up towards his belly. Teddy would time it just right and crouch toward the ground so Rose could land on his lower chest and into his outstretched arms.

"How's my little girl today?" he would ask as she leaped towards him.

"How's my teddy bear?" she would always respond, breaking out into boisterous laughter.

Chaya enjoyed seeing them together because there weren't many men around, and she believed Rose would benefit from having a male figure in her life.

10 | A Shattered Soul

"Mommy, mommy, there's a girl out front by the tree and she's crying and bleeding," yelled out Rose as she tugged at Chaya's skirt to make her follow her.

"Hurry, mommy!"

Chaya ran outside with Rose in tow. She found a fragile teen, bruised and bleeding from a nasty cut on the edge of her mouth. Chaya helped her up and led her inside where she drank several glasses of water.

"What happened to you, my dear child," Chaya asked, expecting the worse.

"I didn't know where else to go, Miss Chaya," said the frightened girl as she wiped the flow of tears. "My Ma beat me so bad when he found out I was carrying Uncle Joe's baby. But he attacked me, Miss Chaya. It wasn't my fault."

The girl started sobbing uncontrollably and Chaya was holding back her own tears.

"My dear child, you didn't do anything wrong. You must be a strong young lady managing to make it all the way here to my home. Now let's get you inside and washed up and put some food into you. Get some rest and we'll talk in the morning."

The young girl, Eve Woods, came from a broken home not too far away and lived in poverty with her parents. Her mother was an abusive alcoholic and her father was barely around. After school one day, she was left alone with her Uncle Joe who was usually too drunk to keep an eye on her anyway. He lost his job at the mill several years back because of his drinking and was never able to get steady work for more than a couple of weeks at a time.

One afternoon, while Eve was going to take a bath, Uncle Joe followed her into the bathroom. He closed the door, and grabbed her from behind with both arms pulling her close to him. Eve could smell the foul stench of whisky on his breath. Uncle Joe threatened to kill her if she screamed, but she shouted out anyways, kicking her legs and struggling to get loose. Uncle Joe was too strong for Eve to fight off and he pushed her down onto the floor and attacked her. It only happened once, but Eve was pregnant and her soul shattered.

Eve was so ashamed that she never told anyone what really happened. In the vicious attack, she was bruised and received numerous cuts and scratches. To explain the injuries and the pain she was in, Eve made up a story about tripping and falling down the stairs while she was carrying her schoolbooks.

Once her belly started showing months later, her mother realized Eve was pregnant and blamed her young daughter. She swung and smacked Eve's face several times causing her mouth to bleed and her cheeks to swell.

"Who could blame Joe after all," she said. Her mother accused Eve of parading her body in front of her uncle and threw her out of the house. The truth was, Eve was an innocent child who'd never even kissed a boy, let alone been touched.

The attack caused her innocence to be forcibly taken and her spirit to be broken.

It took a several months of walks around the ranch and many long conversations with Chaya, for Eve to explain what happened the day she was attacked. Chaya listened with compassion and her heart ached for this young girl. She couldn't imagine the horror Eve went through.

"Miss Chaya, can I ask you something?" Eve asked with her head looking towards the ground, too shy to even look up.

"Of course you can, sweet thing."

"If I have this baby, and it turns out to be a boy, will he be like Uncle Joe? I couldn't bear the thought that my baby might become some animal or something."

"Oh, sweetie, that little angel you're carrying is a child from God. What your uncle did was one of the most terrible things a human being can do to another person, but from this terrible thing, God has sent you an innocent angel. Sometimes when bad things happen, somehow, some good ends up coming from it."

"I know it's not going to be easy, but you have to remember your little baby is just as innocent as you are in all of this. Maybe your child will grow up to save thousands of lives one day. I know keeping the baby will be hard on you, but I'll be right there by your side."

"You don't understand, Miss Chaya, I can't keep this baby. It'll always remind me of what Uncle Joe did to me. I know it's not the baby's fault and all, but I just can't do it. When I stopped by the church on the outskirts of town, Pastor John told me you could help me. He even brought me here to you."

Chaya hadn't thought of Pastor John in years. Who was this Pastor who continued to send these young pregnant girls to her? No one seemed to know a Pastor John at any of the churches, orphanages or help centers around town.

"Why me?" Chaya would ask herself knowing her question would go unanswered. "Why am I being sent these little angels to take care of?" All she knew was that she would be blessed to witness yet another bundle of joy.

Eve delivered a beautiful baby boy she named Alexander. He was born one month premature, but quickly gained weight and was breathing on his own within a couple of weeks. A day after Alexander was home from the hospital, Eve packed her belongings in the middle of the night and was gone by the next morning.

Chaya found a note Eve left asking her to please take care of the baby as her own and saying that she was going to go live in another town with her widowed grandmother, Ellie Sue, who agreed to care for her. Ellie Sue didn't have much in material possessions, but she had a roof over her head, and Eve felt safe there.

Her first letter to Alexander arrived the following year as she had promised Chaya and with the guidance of Ellie Sue, she started working as a receptionist for an abused woman's shelter.

Rose, almost four now, was thrilled to have a baby brother that she could play with and take care of. Alexander had blond curly locks and turquoise big round eyes that melted Chaya's heart, and she couldn't believe her good fortune. The Lord had made up for her loss two times over with these beautiful children.

Rose helped comb the baby's hair every day, sprinkling it with lavender scented baby cologne and she saw to it that Alex's hair was combed just right. Most of the time though, Rose would hold the comb so far away from the baby, fearing she would hurt him if she pressed too hard, that the comb wouldn't even touch his head and Chaya would burst out laughing.

Alex would spend hours quietly staring at everything around him and it was difficult to get his attention. It wasn't until he was several weeks old and examined during a routine doctor visit, that Chaya realized Alex was born almost completely deaf. No amount of noise could get his attention.

At first Chaya was devastated, but she was determined to make sure he led a fulfilling life. She checked out some educational books from the local library and taught herself sign language within a couple of months. She wanted Rose to learn as well, and every day for an hour, Chaya sat with Rose and Alex to teach them the skills they would need in order to communicate not only with each other, but with the rest of the world. Alexander's birth mother, Eve, found out her son was born deaf when she wrote to Chaya and asked how he was doing. Chaya would only respond to the letters if she was asked to out of respect for the birth mothers' privacy.

Although Alexander was rambunctious at times, he was a sweet little boy by nature. One moment he'd be causing some commotion, taking out all the pots and pans from the lower cupboard and dropping them on the floor, and the next he'd walk up to his big sister with an outstretched arm, presenting her with a flower he picked from their garden. As he grew older, Alexander constantly followed Rose, mimicking everything she did with childlike curiosity.

He'd run up to Chaya constantly and hug her, signing that he loved her. Alexander was very detailed and concentrated in everything he did, taking his time to remove his toys from the toy box, playing with them, and then putting them back in the exact same place. Chaya believed he was so detailed because he didn't have the distractions of the hearing world.

There were times she wondered what his world was like. Late at night when the children were finally asleep, Chaya sometimes sat on the floor in the middle of the living room cupping her ears, just looking around.

This is what Alexander saw and heard. This was his perspective of the world.

The silence was deafening.

11 | Going Fishing

*"To be in your children's memory tomorrow, you have
to be in their lives today." ~ Author unknown*

Teddy loved to fish and began to teach Rose how to thread a fishing hook and how to cast the line just right. Rose would sit on her own little wooden chair besides Teddy for hours by the lakeside fishing, and telling stories to each other until sundown.

She stood up and swung the small rod he bought her over her shoulder and catapulted the line into the water before sitting down again. It wasn't long before Rose mastered her fishing technique and every catch was a joyous event shrieking with excitement as if it was her first. As soon as she hooked a fish, Rose would yell for Teddy.

"Teddy, Teddy, I caught one, I caught one!" Rose belted out. Teddy instructed her how to reel in a fish so she wouldn't lose it, but he let Rose do most of the work herself.

"Start pulling up on the rod, Rose," he told her as the fish splashed in and out of the water. "Bring it down slowly, reeling in the line at the same time."

"He's coming, Teddy. I've got him now!"

"That's my girl."

Chaya lay on her blanket playing with Alex just behind them admiring her little extended family. She enjoyed observing Rose and Teddy's fishing adventures and would sketch the two of them for hours on end. These sketches were precious to her and one day, she hoped to write a book about raising adopted children incorporating her own drawings.

On this day, Rose landed three fish all by herself, while Teddy brought in four more by late morning. He helped her grab the flopping fish and take the hooks out of their mouths slipping them into the pail which was full of water to keep them fresh.

"Looks like we got supper already and it's not even noon," Teddy said while staring into the bucket. "We got luck on our side this morning Rose."

"Mommy, come here and look at the fish me and Teddy caught," said Rose proudly as she tugged on Chaya's arm. Chaya got up from her blanket and brought Alex along with her to view the prized catch.

"Honey, you did so well today," Chaya said as Rose pointed inside the pail to the ones she caught.

"Mommy, I caught that one, and that one, and that one, and Teddy caught that one, and that one, and that one, and that one."

Chaya giggled at how Rose was sure she could identify which ones she caught and which ones Teddy brought in even they all looked identical in the pail.

"I agree with you Teddy, I think we've got enough for today," said Chaya as she stared at the fish swimming around in the pail. "Rose has done such a good job that she's become a real pro at catching fish."

Alex was paying close attention to everything that was going on, but he was getting restless so Teddy packed up the chairs, the fishing equipment and the pail as they all headed back home to clean the fish.

Chaya stopped to take one last look around before packing up the blanket and picnic basket while Alex went ahead with Teddy and Rose. The lake had always been a peaceful place for Chaya and it brought many beautiful memories of when she and Michael were together. She missed him at times like these.

12 | The Alden Three

"There is always one moment in childhood when the door opens and lets the future in." - *Deepak Chopra*

As another summer drew to an end, the neighborhood children were determined to outplay each other until they were called in for supper and Jennifer Alden could outplay them all. Having three older brothers, and learning to keep up with the boys, was truly a matter of survival for Jennifer.

Benjamin III, the oldest brother, had just become interested in girls and fast cars and he usually hung out at the pizzeria on Bird Road where the high school crowd met in the parking lot after school. Cameron, ten, and Devon who was nine, were closer in age to Jennifer. Her brothers took her along with them almost everywhere they went, but not necessarily by choice. Sometimes they were on what the boys would call 'guard duty,' courtesy of their mother Katherine.

Although they sometimes whined about having to take care of their little sister, the boys were very protective of her, and in the neighborhood, this dynamic trio were called, the Alden Three. At six years old, Jennifer was an awkward child, always getting hurt while playing football with the older boys. It was a common sight to see her walking home with tears streaming down her dirt-covered face, cradling her elbow or knee to soothe an injury, but all the boys wanted Jennifer on their team because she was a fast runner and a true and fierce competitor who could swing around the taller boys just out of their reach.

For all the toughness she portrayed on the playground, Jennifer was terrified of returning to school after the summer break. Her first year did not go so well, and this year she'd be entering the second grade at the same elementary school. Jennifer had a slight stutter so her teacher suggested to her parents to place her in a special class for children with speech impediments at the school.

After discussing it with the school counselor and receiving approval from Jennifer's parents, her teacher Mrs. Brentworth placed her in the Special Education Class called the SEC for one hour each day. There were four other children in the SEC class with impediments, so Jennifer didn't feel so alone, and in fact, the class turned out to be an escape for her from the taunting she was being subjected to by the school bully.

The children were instructed to play various educational vocal games while the teacher monitored their progress. Other times they told each other stories, both real and make-believe, and boy, could Jennifer tell some fancy stories!

Jennifer's stories would always begin with the same line, "a long, long, time ago there was a beautiful p, p, princess and a very handsome tall p, p, prince who…" The stories would change, but they always began in the exact same manner. Although Jennifer was only six and a half years old, she was a true romantic at heart and in her eyes every woman was a princess, and every man, a prince.

But this escape in the secure environment of the special class was short-lived. When she returned to her regular class during fifth period, the ridiculing continued.

"Jennifer, ca ca can you t-t-t-talk better now," the class bully named Tom would say to her. Jennifer's eyes would swell with tears, but she was slowly learning to ignore him.

Seeing the fear in her little girl's eyes before going to school, each and every morning Jennifer's mother would take her aside, holding both her hands in hers and say, "Now Jen, you're a big strong girl. You've got to stand up for yourself. You are very special and don't you ever forget that!"

What began as a daily morning lecture became Jennifer's mantra. Whenever she got into an uncomfortable situation she would chant the words, "I'm very special. I'm very special." Surprisingly however, the new school year turned out to be somewhat pleasant and Jennifer found second grade to be much kinder overall than her first school year. With the help of her special class teacher, her stuttering improved dramatically, and the kids became friendlier towards her. By year's end she had made some new close friends and her confidence was beginning to take a whole new turn.

13 | Mother's Day 1954

"It's so good to know that wherever you are a mom is with you in spirit and in love." ~ Author unknown

Dear Summer,

You must be getting so big now that you're almost eight years old. How are you doing in school my sweetheart? Do you have many friends? Do you like your teachers? I wonder what captures your interest and what talents you have. Do you like to draw like me or are you more like your father?

How do you like to wear your hair? Is your hair short or long now like Rose's hair? Does your mother comb it and put it in pigtails or do you tie it back in a ponytail? Is your hair reddish like mine or blond like your daddy?

If only I could have a little window into your life to see and experience what your life is like and to reassure myself that you are happy, healthy and well cared for. That's really all I want in this world…to know that you are okay. You can't imagine the thoughts that run in my head, second guessing my decision to place you with another family. My heart aches for you every single day of my life.

Do you know you also have a little brother now? His name is Alexander, but we call him Alex. Alex was born deaf, but I am teaching him sign language so he can learn to communicate with us and we're also learning to communicate with him.

Alex is so full of spirit and a joy to be around. He follows your little sister Rose around all the time trying to mimic everything she does. It's so darling, it just makes my heart flutter. I know Rose would be looking up to you as her big sister if you were here with us.

I remember when Rose took her first steps. It was so exciting! Oh how I wish I could have seen your first steps Summer. Your face must have lit up the room just like little Rose's did. What did you hold on to my little one? Did you grab the coffee table, or did you hold on to your Mother's hand? I was right there beside you honey in spirit and I know you must have looked so proud of your new accomplishment. I would have been beaming with joy to be able to see that.

Do you have any brothers and sisters? I hope you do and I hope you have a lot of friends to play with. Are you okay, my angel? Does your Mother tuck you in at night and do your parents read you stories and kiss you goodnight on your forehead?

I tuck you in every night my sweetheart. That kiss you feel on your forehead before you fall asleep is me, my darling. Remember to close your eyes whenever you need me, wrap your arms around yourself, and I'll be hugging you right back.

I love you, my angel…sweet dreams,

Mommy

14 | Time Is A Gift

*"You cannot add more minutes to the day, but you
can utilize each one to the fullest."*
~ Menachem Mendel Schneerson

Jennifer idolized her father Benjamin and she imitated many things he did. A self-taught man, Benjamin read over two hundred books by the time he was eighteen years old. Left fatherless at age six, Benjamin went to work in his early teens at odd jobs to help support his mother, Francis. Nothing came easy and there was little time to play.

"Never give up, Jennifer, and always work hard to your fullest potential," he'd say to her constantly. This provided her with a competitive edge that Jennifer took advantage of as she was growing up.

Benjamin expected a lot from his children and he wasn't afraid to let them know it. He struggled through his youth, saving every penny he could and what started out as a little clothing store Benjamin opened, turned out to be a major retail chain that eventually allowed the family to live a comfortable, respectable life.

Benjamin was a handsome man with a gentle soul standing at six feet four inches tall, and ever since Jennifer could remember, he had a head full of thick salt and pepper hair. He wore it slicked back with hair grease and although his round gold-rimmed spectacles seemed too small for his face, it gave him a very distinguished look with his strong square jaw and chiseled chin.

A gold pocket watch constantly dangled from Benjamin's black leather belt and into his left side trouser pocket. As a young girl, Jennifer enjoyed following the thin intricate gold chain from his waist with her fingers slipping her hand into his trouser pocket and yanking out the pocket watch. She got a thrill from pressing the small button on top as she watched the cover fling open. Jennifer then snapped it shut, put it back into his trouser pocket, and did it over and over again until she finally tired. This little game brought a smile to Benjamin's face no matter how busy or occupied he was. He took advantage of the game to teach Jennifer at least one new thought or lesson each day.

"Daddy, it's twelve, twenty four," Jennifer said after opening his watch.

"You've mastered reading the time very well and very quickly, Jen," Ben replied.

Jennifer learned to tell time by the age of two. Not only could she read the time of day, but she could tell how many hours remained in the day. Benjamin was determined to instill into Jennifer, who was always fascinated with time, how precious this commodity was. He taught her to take heed and live every day to its fullest for that particular day only came once in her lifetime. To take a moment out of each day and stop to look around at the people you love; to smell the different aromas that nature offered; to look at the plants and the sky and appreciate their beauty.

"Never take anything for granted Jennifer," he said, stating today's lesson. "What you have today may not be there tomorrow, but you should never be sad about that, for each tomorrow brings new things you didn't have today. Treasure everything you have every single day and you won't have any regrets in the future."

On this day Benjamin's lesson was coming from a painful past experience. It had been thirty-three years to the day since his father suddenly died of a heart attack while working in the field behind their house. It was a young Benjamin who found his father face down by the fence post and he grabbed his father's shirt around the arm and with all his might, tried to roll him over onto his back.

He never forgot the look of death he saw in his father's eyes that tragic day. Although he was just a boy, Benjamin knew it was too late to revive him, since his uncle had that same cold stare when he passed away almost a year earlier. Benjamin closed his own teary eyes, clenched his fists up to his chest and tilted his head towards the sky. He could not restrain himself any longer and let out a bellow that could be heard far away.

"Nooo, God, nooo!" he screamed at the top of his lungs. "Don't take my father away! Don't take him."

Overcome with grief, he collapsed on top of his father, his arms hugging the lifeless body. With each sob his body jerked as his tears soaked into his father's dirt covered shirt.

Within minutes, Benjamin's mother Margaret ran outside and found the two loves of her life slumped together in the field. Her son's screams had led her to them and it took all her strength to pull Benjamin away from his father.

She had known this day would come, since the doctor said he had a bad heart and should stop working so hard, but her husband was an honorable man who was intent on taking care of his family. Even so, she was never really prepared for this day to arrive and watching Benjamin's grief stricken, teary red face, broke her heart even more.

"Mommy, why did God take Daddy away from us?" asked Benjamin gasping for air.

"Oh Benji, I wish I knew the answer," his mother replied trying to comfort him. "Your father was such a good man that I guess God decided he needed him in heaven."

"But Mom," he answered, "God never gave me a chance to say good-bye. He didn't give me a chance to tell Daddy how much I loved him. He was the best father a kid could ask for."

Margaret pulled him closer to her chest and wrapped her loving arms around her boy. "Benji," his mother began. "Your father knew with all his soul how much you loved him. You made him so proud. Every time you look up into the sky, think of your father. His spirit will always be with you. He will be guiding us and looking out for us the rest of our lives. Always know that, and let that thought comfort you when you are sad. Let it bring a smile to your face in the good times too. Take a moment every day and think about everything and everyone in your life, for tomorrow it may not be there."

"Benji, your life will always be changing. People will come in and out of your life, but for everyone that leaves, something even better will come into your life. Live life to its fullest every day and you will have no regrets."

"Do the best you can and grow up to be an honest, respectable man like your Daddy was. That's all we could ever hope for you Benji and don't ever forget how much we both love you."

Margaret placed a gentle kiss on his forehead and led him back to the house.

"I love you Mommy," Benjamin said with a slight grin.

"Daddy, Daddy. Are you listening to me?" Jennifer's question snapped Benjamin back from his childhood memories.

"What, sweetheart?" Benjamin asked as a tear streamed down his cheek. He wasn't able to wipe it away in time before Jennifer noticed it. "I'm sorry. I didn't hear you. What were you saying?"

"Daddy, why are you crying?" she asked. "Are you sad because you have regrets?"

"Jen, even though I've tried to live my life so your grandma and grandpa would be proud...you see, my father died when I was about your age and I never got a chance to tell him how much I loved him. So sometimes it saddens me a little, but that's not going to happen with us and the boys because I'm going to let you know every day how much I love all of you."

Benjamin bent down and scooped her up with his outstretched arms, twirling her round and round like she loved for him to do while Jennifer giggled with laughter.

15 | Love Has No Color

Fall turned to winter, and Chaya had just put Rose and Alex to bed for a nap when the doorbell rang.

"Excuse me, are you Chaya Rose?" said a girl wearing a velvet blue jacket and shivering uncontrollably.

"You must be freezing out there, please come in," said Chaya as she led the visitor into her home while a truck sped away from the driveway. "Yes I'm Chaya Rose. What can I do for you?"

"I just came into town with my pa and a Pastor at one of the local churches told us I should come see you," explained the girl.

"Don't tell me, was his name Pastor John?"

"Yes. As a matter of fact it was. He said you help young ladies who are in special situations and I don't know what to do. I want my baby so much, but I can't keep it. My father works at the mill in the small town where we live and we barely make due. I have five other siblings and we just can't afford another mouth to feed so, although I would love to be able to keep my baby, I decided it's best to place him or her for adoption."

Chaya couldn't believe it was happening all over again. Who was this Pastor John who was sending these lost souls to her?

"Mommy, I can't sleep," said Rose as she slowly made her way down the stairs rubbing her eyes.

"It's okay, sweetheart. Come here, I want you to meet a new friend."

"Oh, I'm sorry, my name is Patricia…Patricia Williams," said the young black girl with the short cropped afro. "She's beautiful. What's her name?"

"Her name is Rose," said the proud mother as she pulled her up onto her hip. "Rose Summer Stuart. She is beautiful isn't she? You made the right choice Patricia in coming here and I'm glad you have chosen to have this baby and place it for adoption."

Patricia stayed in the same room as Heather and Eve did before her, since it still had the old rocking chair in it. The room was decorated with beautiful curtains and a hand-made quilt bedspread that Chaya's mother had sewn many years ago making it cozy and perfect for guests.

For several months, Patricia helped with the chores and entertained Rose and Alex while Chaya prepared the daily meals. Chaya and Patricia got along well for they both enjoyed reading, taking long walks, and playing with the children.

After feeling very tired one evening, Patricia began experiencing some minor labor pains. Chaya kept a watchful eye on her, placing cold compresses on Patricia's forehead, and stayed constantly by her side throughout the night. By morning, the labor pains were getting stronger and Chaya placed a call to the local obstetrician, Dr. Smathers.

By the time the doctor arrived a few hours later, Patricia was minutes from giving birth and after numerous commands from the doctor to push hard, Patricia gave birth to a seven pound, six ounce healthy baby boy.

The first time Chaya held him, she knew in her heart that Rose and Alex were going to have a baby brother. Patricia named him Kendrick Allen II after the father he would never know. "That'll be all he has of his father beside his good looks," said a tearful Patricia, as she held him close to her.

Patricia stayed with Chaya only two more days after giving birth fearing it would be too hard to leave her baby the more time she spent with him. Chaya's eyes welled up as Patricia handed the baby to her, because she knew how hard this was for her. Chaya promised to take good care of him and she reassured Patricia she was welcome to come and stay with them anytime she wanted. She always encouraged the birth mothers to stay in touch with their children and Patricia was comforted by that thought, and also with the possibility of visiting Kendrick in the future when she was ready to.

She contacted her father the night before so he could come pick her up the following morning. Patricia's father, Thomas Williams, waited on the porch for his daughter to come outside. He tipped his hat while nodding downward after Chaya opened the front door, but kept his distance, fearing if he came any closer, Chaya would see the tears in his eyes.

Although he kept his stoic appearance, Chaya felt Mr. Williams was aching to see his first grandson. Patricia gave Chaya and her son one last kiss and hurried out the front door carrying her small suitcase towards her father. Just as Mr. Williams turned to leave, Kendrick burst into an ear-wrenching wail and although he hesitated for a moment, Mr. Williams tipped his hat one more time, turned, and walked toward his pickup truck behind his daughter. Chaya hoped he would have asked to see his grandson at least once, but it was not to be.

Her life was difficult when she returned home, but two years later, Patricia enrolled at the community college with the money she earned at her part-time job and babysitting on weekends. Mr. Williams discouraged his daughter from ever mentioning the baby again thinking that it was best for Patricia, but Kendrick was always on her mind and in her heart.

Patricia wrote to Kendrick the following Mother's Day as she had promised, and Chaya anxiously looked forward to her letter, since she had been concerned about Patricia's wellbeing. Chaya put away the letter she received in a wooden box she constructed herself out of cherry wood back in the old barn with her father's tools. On the lid, Chaya hand carved Kendrick's full birth name, his date of birth, and the names of both his birth mother and his natural father. One day when the time was right, he too, would know the 'whys.'

16 | Running For Office

Jennifer excelled not only scholastically in school, but socially as well and became rather popular. The physical aptitude she gained as a child playing with her brothers, always seemed to land her as team captain on the playing field at school. This newfound leadership role captivated Jennifer, and she thrived on the attention while the girls began looking up to her with adulation.

Jennifer had grown up to be a tall, athletic, intelligent young lady full of confidence. It was only natural when she got to the sixth grade that she ran for the position of class president, even though there was stiff competition since she overheard that Cody, the best looking and tallest boy in the class, was planning to run for president too.

Cody was infatuated with Jennifer from the moment he laid his eyes on her at a school event. Although they had become friends, Cody hoped for a closer relationship, but his subtle attempts at courtship never elicited more than a sweet smile from Jennifer. Her eyes had been set on Scotty, a blonde-haired, handsome boy with a pearl-white grin and big beautiful hazel eyes enveloped with the longest thickest eyelashes she had ever seen.

Cody found out from several of his schoolmates that Jennifer liked Scotty, and now to top it off, he heard a rumor that Jennifer wanted to run for the same office as him; the presidency.

"How could this happen to me, Greg?" Cody asked his best friend in disbelief. "How could I possibly campaign against my beautiful Jennifer? She will never speak to me again if I win. Even worse, what would she think of me if I lose? That I was a wimp? A loser?" The thought made him shiver.

Mrs. Hart, Jennifer's sixth grade teacher, had to raise her voice in order to capture the attention of the restless class. "All right children, settle down now," she yelled out, flailing her arms in an attempt to round up the kids like a herd of cattle. "Everyone please take your seats."

After weeks of speculation, the kids were anxious to learn who was going to run for their class president, and the time had finally arrived. For Mrs. Hart, this event was an important one and she enjoyed this time of the school year when the election nominations began. The democratic system of electing officials had always fascinated her and she wanted her students to learn and experience the process.

"Please, everyone have a seat so we can get started," she pleaded to the class. After explaining that in order to be an official candidate you had to be nominated and another person had to second the motion, Greg's hand went up in a flash.

"Mrs. Hart, Mrs. Hart!" Greg was yelling out with his arm raised high in the air, swinging back and forth.

"Yes, Greg," Mrs. Hart responded quickly hoping to calm Greg's anxiousness. "What would you like to say?"

"I would like to nominate my very good friend and the next class president, Cody Thompson." Upon hearing that, cheers went out and the class went wild. When Mrs. Hart asked if anyone would like to second the motion, not just one, but half the class responded and Mrs. Hart was elated at all the enthusiasm.

"Okay kids, we have one official nomination, so is there anyone else who would like to make a nomination?" she asked while scanning the room for a raised hand. In the back of the room, little freckle faced Claire Peters shyly raised her hand.

"Claire, do you want to nominate someone?" Mrs. Hart asked while trying to encourage her knowing that she was very timid and it was difficult for her to speak up in class.

"Yes Mrs. Hart," Claire uttered in a small squeaky voice. "I would like to nominate the greatest friend anyone could have. I'd like to nominate Jennifer Alden." And with that announcement the class cheered and roared, and also moved to quickly second the nomination.

Although Cody and Jennifer had amassed quite a following since they were both very personable and popular with their classmates, Mrs. Hart asked if there were any more nominations to be made, but it seemed the class had rehearsed their response when they replied in unison, "No, Mrs. Hart."

On that note, Mrs. Hart officially congratulated both Cody and Jennifer before reciting the campaign rules. Above all, it was to be fair. No name-calling and no cheating, and each candidate was to campaign on his or her own merits and present to their classmates how they were going to best represent them among all the other classes in their grade.

Jennifer was so excited she couldn't wait to get home and tell her family, especially her father. She pictured the look of pride on his face after her announcement that his little Jen would be president of her sixth grade class.

"Daddy, Daddy!" Jennifer yelled out as she came running up the driveway.

"Calm down, Jen," her father said in his warm way as she jumped onto his lap as he sat in his chair on the porch. "Calm down and catch your breath. Now tell me what in world is going on with you?"

"I've been chosen president of my class, Daddy. Well, first I have to beat Cody of course, but that should be easy. You see, I counted, and there are more girls than boys in the class, and all the girls said they would vote for me. I've got it in the bag!" Jennifer explained to her father with her chest arched forward.

"Is that so, Jen?" her father asked with curiosity. "You've got this all figured out, do you? Tell me something, Jen. How many more girls are there than boys in this class of yours?"

"Well, counting me, there are sixteen girls and there are only fifteen boys counting Cody," answered Jennifer, bewildered at the question.

"So what you're telling me is, if there were sixteen boys, counting Cody of course, and only fifteen girls counting you, then Cody would be the next class president instead of you?" Ben surmised.

"Well yes, I guess you could say that," Jennifer replied cautiously. "But that's not the case Daddy. There's more girls in my class and that's all there is to it."

Jennifer was confused. She thought her father would be overjoyed, but he didn't appear to be. "What's wrong?" she asked herself. "Why was he asking all these questions?"

"Aren't you happy for me, Daddy?" Jennifer asked with a puzzled look on her face.

"Of course I am, sweetheart. I just want to give you a little something to think about. What if for instance, there were more boys than girls in your class, Jen? Wouldn't you want to be given a chance to campaign on an equal playing field? Wouldn't you want to be able to tell your fellow students what you can offer them and be given a chance to win based on your merits, instead of winning because there are more girls than boys in your class or vice versa? Aren't you going to feel better if you win because you, Jennifer Alden, will be a better president than your challenger, whoever that may be?"

"Jen, women have struggled to better themselves and get a college education. Whether you decide to marry and have a family after you graduate high school, or go on to college, or follow a career first, a person should be judged on their merits and their merits alone. Not by their gender, or their race, or for any other reason. When I look at you Jen, I see a beautiful young girl with a tough road ahead. I see stumbling blocks that some in society will try to put in your way. Not because you are a bad person or you don't deserve to get ahead, but simply because you are a female. It isn't right and it definitely isn't fair, but unfortunately, sometimes you may need to prove yourself twice as hard as a man would have to."

"Hopefully, one day our society will move beyond these prejudices and respect everyone equally, but until then, prove yourself. Win this presidency because you are Jennifer Alden, and you bring good ideas and leadership, not because there are sixteen girls and fifteen boys in your class. Win because you deserve it."

Jennifer was at a loss for words and the admiration she had for her father's wisdom had never been greater. Her eyes began to overflow with tears as she placed her long slender arms around her father's neck and kissed his cheek.

"I love you, Daddy," she said with a grin.

"I love you too, Jen."

17 | More Bundles of Joy

"You don't choose your family. They are God's gift to you,
as you are to them." ~ Desmond Tutu

As the years went by, Chaya became a mother to four more children. There was Amanda, a precocious and bright little girl who took over Alex's attention from Rose. Her mother, Samantha, came to Chaya's home in her eighth month of pregnancy and although she was torn about giving up her baby, she knew her child would be in a safe home with brothers and sisters, and a wonderful mother who would adore her baby.

Then there was Jack and Jordon, identical twins whose young mother, Amy, already had two other children she could barely take care of. Amy had been abandoned by her husband at nineteen and was already working two jobs to support her young daughters, Jasmin and Laura. After much contemplating and speaking with her Pastor, Amy was led to Chaya's home. Born just three minutes apart, Jack and Jordon became Chaya's fifth and sixth child. Sarah was born to Anne Marie just one year later and became Chaya's seventh adopted child.

Rose was turning out to be quite a young lady, always anxious to help out with the children and never complained.

She would make sure all the children were up and dressed before breakfast and this help gave Chaya the time to home school her ever growing brood. Rose would also help the children with their daily homework lesson and got them bathed and ready for supper.

Alex was excelling in all subjects and mastering lip reading as well. Whenever Teddy stopped by the house, Alex worked with him mouthing words over and over and then signing them back. Teddy developed a real fondness for Alex, not because of his deafness, but because he was such a kind and gentle soul, and the feeling was mutual.

Kendrick's skin color was never brought up by the children as he fit right in with the family. Kendrick saw Teddy as a father figure and he believed Teddy was his own father because the color of Teddy's skin matched his own. Teddy knew it was wrong not to correct him, but he enjoyed this attention, and he loved being called Dad, something he never got to experience before. Chaya didn't encourage it, but she didn't discourage it either. She told Kendrick he had a birth father, but that if he wanted to, he could also call Teddy his Dad and this made Kendrick feel special believing he had two fathers. In fact, Teddy became a father figure to all of the children and a good close friend to Chaya who supported her emotionally and gave her advice when she needed it.

18 | The Vote

*"Voting is the expression of our commitment to ourselves,
one another, this country and this world."*
~ Sharon Salzberg

It was a hard-fought campaign, and now the moment of truth had come, so Mrs. Hart called the class to order. Although Jennifer tried to campaign on her beliefs and ideas, the unofficial count among her friends still showed all the girls voting for her and all the boys voting for Cody. It just didn't seem fair to Jennifer since Cody proved to be an honorable competitor and even had some fresh ideas Jennifer thought complimented her campaign.

"It just isn't right," she murmured to herself, thinking what her father told her when he found out she was nominated to be the class president. "It's so unfair. He will never have a chance. I tried Daddy. I really tried."

Mrs. Hart passed a ballot to every student and gave instructions to vote for either Mr. Cody Thompson or Miss Jennifer Alden by circling either name on the ballot. After making their choice, the students were told to fold the paper twice in half so their vote would be confidential. Mrs. Hart went around to each student with a small plastic bowl and collected all thirty-one ballots. One by one, each student anxiously dropped their official ballot into the bowl as Mrs. Hart walked by. Once all the ballots were collected, Mrs. Hart went to the front of the classroom and drew a vertical line on the blackboard.

On one side she wrote Jennifer's name and on the other, she wrote Cody. Mrs. Hart slowly reached into the bowl to retrieve the first ballot and marked it on the blackboard with a short line on Cody's side. You could hear a pin drop as she reached for the second ballot and marked a line on Jennifer's side of the blackboard. As the count went on, it appeared it was going to be a very close race as all the boys spontaneously began gathering around Cody and all the girls surrounded Jennifer.

As the ballots dwindled down in the bowl, the voting was turning out to be just about even. Number 28, Cody. 29, Jennifer. 30, Jennifer. There was one more ballot left in the bowl and the score was a dead tie.

Cody's heart sank, knowing deep down that there weren't enough boys in the class to sway the vote, because his unofficial count showed fifteen boys would vote for him, and sixteen girls would vote for Jennifer and the only thing he could hope for was for one of the girls to come over to his side. As Mrs. Hart slowly opened the last ballot, a smile came to Jennifer's face. "It's not circled!" Mrs. Hart exclaimed a little stunned.

"What?" yelled the students. "That can't be!"

"Settle down everyone!" Mrs. Hart said in a loud, firm voice. "Someone obviously did not vote." It suddenly dawned on Mrs. Hart that in her instruction to the students on how to cast their vote, she failed to mention that one can abstain.

To be sure someone didn't forget to circle their vote, the teacher asked each student, one by one, if they had voted the way they intended to. One by one, everyone said they had. Having satisfied her doubt, Mrs. Hart turned around to look at the blackboard one more time and recounted the marks.

She slowly turned to face the class, took a deep long breath and declared a tie. For the first time in the school's history, a class would have co-presidents. Cody couldn't believe his ears. He'd been so sure he was doomed, that he didn't realize the boys were lifting him up into the air. Jennifer was also being surrounded and lifted into the air by all the girls in the class.

Mrs. Hart was speechless for the first time in her life. She was intrigued, and after the commotion died down a bit, Mrs. Hart gathered the two co-presidents and congratulated them. Mrs. Hart knew someone purposely abstained, and she wondered who it could have been and more importantly, why?

As Jennifer left the classroom that afternoon she went over to Mrs. Hart's desk and slipped her a note. In it she wrote: "You shouldn't win something just because you are a girl or a boy. You should win because you deserve it. We both deserved it."

19 | Mother's Day 1962
Sweet Sixteen

"At sixteen, the world is yours to have. You can do,
you can be, anything you put your mind to."
~ Author unknown

Dear Summer,

Within a year you'll be turning sweet sixteen. How beautiful you must be. I hope your parents are able to give you a big birthday party to celebrate this wonderful milestone. Have you picked out a special dress to wear already? Are you inviting all your friends to your party? I hope you are surrounded by a loving family and that you have many good friends by your side who really care about you.

Is there a special boy in your life? I wish I could be there with you to explain about love and boys, and how you should be careful now that you're becoming a young woman.

Summer, I hope you make a wiser choice than I did. I don't know if your adoptive mother has spoken to you about boys and taking precautions. I hope you wait to have relations with a young man until you're married and can provide a good home to a child.

You know, no one expects to become pregnant, but they do, and then your life can turn upside down.

When I was sixteen, even though your father and I took some precautions, I became pregnant with you, my darling. As you know, my father would have none of it, and in order not to shame my parents, I left town until I delivered you. When I looked at you as you took your first breath, I thought to myself, "Now how in the world can this possibly be a 'mistake'?

I know I should have waited to have relations with your father until we were legally married and older and wiser, but we didn't, and I paid the consequences. Know that you have both of our souls within you and you are the result of two people who loved each other tremendously.

You were, and are, so wanted, my darling. Please know that. I don't know if I'll ever get a chance to meet you, or if you'll ever read the letters that I write to you every year, but I want you to know how very much I love and miss you. I hope you're not mad at me for placing you with a good family, and I hope you understand.

Your adopted brothers and sisters have grown up so much and they've blossomed into beautiful souls. I have seven children now and they are such a blessing. Oh how I would have wanted to raise you. Sometimes the pain is unbearable, but I have faith that you are okay, and that I did the right thing at that time. Happy sweet sixteen my sweetheart.

I love you my Summer,

Mommy

20 | Pursuing Dreams

"I'll love you until the day after forever."
~Author unknown

Jennifer graduated high school with honors and won a scholarship to the renowned Art Institute in Atlanta. Although her parents encouraged her to explore her talents, Jennifer hesitated at the thought of leaving not only her family behind, but also her loving beau, Brian Taylor, and Brian wasn't keen on Jennifer leaving so soon after finally winning her heart.

Brian was a very handsome, tall, well-built young man with short-cropped curly blonde hair. Although they had been friends throughout high school, it wasn't until they ended up at the same party one night that they both realized their friendship was turning into something more. For Brian, their relationship was the culmination of years of admiration and for Jennifer, it was a welcomed, but unexpected surprise.

Six months passed since their first date, and it was increasingly difficult to simply kiss and say goodnight.

"I love you so much, Jen," Brian would often tell her while holding her cheeks in his hands. "I don't know what I would do without you."

One evening in the middle of the night, Brian ran more than five miles from his house to hers just to knock on her bedroom window and whisper "goodnight, my love" to her. He was notorious for staging surprises, and stunts like that stole her heart. Brian begged Jennifer not to leave for Atlanta, but he realized the art institute was where she dreamed of going, so he reluctantly gave her his blessing.

"Oh Brian, I'm going to miss you so much," Jennifer said with tears streaming down her face. "Maybe I should go to the local community college for a while and then transfer to the art institute in a couple of years? Maybe you can come with me?" Jennifer was grasping at straws to figure out how they could stay together and still follow their dreams.

Brian couldn't leave his recently widowed mother and three younger brothers alone and being the oldest, he was the glue that held his family together. His brothers looked up to him and his mother needed a man around the house to keep the boys in line and to help with fixing things.

"Hush, my Jennifer," whispered Brian as he put his loving fingers over her sweet pouting lips. "Jen, if our love is as strong as it feels, nothing will separate us no matter how many miles are between you and me. You'll only be less than four hours away, and whenever I get time off from work, I'll take the bus to Atlanta and we'll spend our weekends together until you graduate."

"Oh Brian, the thought of not being with you is driving me crazy," Jennifer responded anxiously. "You don't know how much I truly love you and depend on you as my support."

"I know Jen and I feel the same about you. We'll get through this and we'll still talk to each other all the time by telephone and see each other often, I promise."

The time was nearing when Jennifer was set to leave for Atlanta. In a couple of days, she would begin a new life in a new school, in a new town and meet new friends. Although she didn't want to leave, Jennifer also felt an exciting change was about to take place and she was ready for the challenge.

On their last night together, Brian and Jennifer decided to go to their favorite isolated spot by a lake in a park where they could be alone with only the sounds of nature and with each other under the stars. It was a beautiful moonlit evening, and the air had the sweet smell of blooming flowers. Jennifer was a bundle of mixed emotions and as they lay on their quilted blanket side by side, they made a promise to each other; that their love would be forever.

Jennifer pulled Brian closer to her and they passionately kissed and caressed each other for a long while. She suddenly stopped for a moment to gaze into his eyes, pulling his body over hers with an embrace so strong she felt his body would go right through hers. Their screams of pleasure broke the still of the night, and they would never forget this evening of passion for the rest of their lives. On that night, they became one.

21 | The Children Blossom

"There is a garden in every childhood, an enchanted place where colors are brighter, the air softer, and the morning more fragrant than ever again."
~ Elizabeth Lawrence

The children were growing fast, and Rose was beginning to come into her own. She continued to help Chaya tremendously, looking after the children especially Amanda the youngest, the twins who were a handful, and little Sarah. The younger children usually waited for Rose by the door to go out to the barn and play hide and seek, run after the animals, or just rummage through the old crates, making up games as they went along.

Rose continued to help with the chores around the house and help Chaya prepare the evening supper. She enjoyed cooking from an early age, and had recently started creating her own recipes with the encouragement of her mother. But Chaya also insisted Rose go out and play for at least an hour first before allowing her to help around the house.

Rose turned out to be a real character, and she loved to entertain the younger children with her barnyard tea parties. She would make up a storyline in order to hold the twins' attention as much as possible and assign the children roles to play. The stories the children came up with would always make Rose burst with laughter. Eventually, the boys would get tired and start demolishing the beautiful table Rose laid out.

Alex was growing up and looking to develop his hobbies into a profitable venture to make some spending money. Alex, whose deafness never held him back, was expanding his artistic talent and began making portable herb gardens with the handpicked plants he'd find around the property. Whenever Teddy came upon some discarded wooden trays from the local hardware and grocery stores, he collected them for Alex, and one by one, Alex filled them with soil and began creating his masterpieces.

As he got older, the "pods," as he'd call them, got fancier and fancier. In one corner of the pod, he built a layered mountain of rock he'd sculpt with a small pick and hammer. To bind them together, he mixed a batch of plaster and carefully bonded each rock, one slightly further back than the other creating a small mountain terrain.

Each pod had its unique corner rock formation, a variety of herbal and decorative plants, an intricate small wooden two-plank bench he constructed himself, instructions on the care of the pod and his signature trademark boulder with his name painted on it. When Alex finished a half dozen or so pods, Teddy drove him into town exhibiting them from the back of his pickup truck and within a couple of hours, Alex usually sold them all to passersby.

His talent was undeniable, and he was starting to be known around town as "the Pod Kid." Over time, his garden creations grew into full-fledged works of art and nurseries and local shops began asking Alex to place his creations in their stores on consignment. They did so well, the storeowners finally starting placing regular monthly orders and Alex was able to put away some well-earned money. All this attention and success didn't distract Alex from perfecting his work and the pride he displayed in his pods and the intricate nature of his creations, kept him focused and humble.

Chaya was very proud of Alex and all he had accomplished, but before he was allowed to work on his pods, she insisted he finish all his homework first and set aside time to play with his siblings. Maybe it was the silence his world offered that allowed Alex to mentally flourish and express himself with his garden pods. He had an uncanny ability to bring out the details nature provided, that few people ever took the time to notice.

Kendrick, who was three years younger than Alex, followed suit in his own special way. Kendrick was enthralled with building things, and he would search around the ranch for his own scraps of wood and build boxes or small chests. His designs were intricate for his age, but he was able to follow through from his original drawings he sketched, to the finished product.

For his larger projects that needed some heavier power tools, Kendrick enlisted the help of Teddy for guidance. It wasn't long before Kendrick learned how to use most of the wood working tools in the barn, and with Teddy's supervision, Kendrick was able to operate them himself. Together they built dozens of pieces of furniture that he and Teddy sold in town, allowing Kendrick to save money towards a college education. He aspired to be an architect one day, and Teddy took pride in helping him towards achieving that goal.

22 | The Bus Trip

"Love is composed of a single soul inhabiting two bodies."
~ Aristotle

As the final class let out for the day, Jennifer made plans to meet two of her college school mates, Christie and Johanna, later that evening at their on-campus hangout known as The Rat. Even though over nine weeks had passed since she had been with Brian and had "become a woman," every time she passed by a mirror she swore she saw a glow of light surround her reflection. But lately, Jennifer felt a little run down and all the excitement of moving into her new apartment and organizing her schedule was beginning to take a physical toll on her.

When she arrived at The Rat that evening to meet her friends, they were waiting for her at their favorite corner booth. Christie, an aspiring fashion designer who wanted to open her own clothing boutique one day, and Johanna, who was known as the "film master" and whose dream was to be a professional videographer and film editor, made a natural trio with Jennifer, the talented artist. Each of them had moved away from their hometown leaving behind family and friends to attend the Art

Institute and the three instantly bonded during an orientation session weeks before school began. They moved into the same popular apartment building near the campus that mainly housed students, each leaving behind boyfriends they longed to be with.

Even though they had come from stable and close loving families, the trio was remarkably independent. Each had a strong character, were very creative and not fearful of taking on the future. The yearning to be successful at their talents gave them the confidence they needed to face the uncertainty of what lied ahead in their lives.

Growing up, Jennifer always strived to be successful at whatever she did and the she would often think of the time when she ran for class president in the sixth grade, and how that experience shaped her into the woman she was today. Jennifer instantly felt at home with her new friends since they reminded her of her childhood when she was known as one of the Alden Three and the thought of her brothers and that special time of childhood innocence always brought a smile to her face.

She arrived at The Rat that evening completely famished because with everything that was going on, Jennifer had forgotten to eat lunch. Brian phoned early in the morning to say he was aching to see her and to get directions to her new apartment complex, planning to ride the early morning bus the following day. Jennifer was ecstatic and had worked all day on the apartment, finishing some painting that needed to be done and organizing, to prepare for Brian's arrival and now, she looked forward to unwinding with her friends before going back home.

"He's coming tomorrow," Jennifer said with excitement to her friends. "Brian's coming and I can't wait. It's been over two months, and I miss him so much. I'm dying for you girls to meet him."

"Oh Jen, you're so lucky," responded Johanna with a little envy in her voice. "My Johnny can't visit me for at least another month."

"And Kevin can't get away from his new job for another eight weeks until the holiday weekend," Christie followed with disappointment in her voice. "You're one lucky girl Jennifer Alden."

Later that evening, Jennifer made sure her alarm clock was set early enough so she wouldn't arrive late at the bus station. Thoughts of her last night with Brian were replaying in her mind like a movie on a never-ending reel, and she had a surprise for him.

Early in their relationship, she envisioned that making love to Brian would be a beautiful experience, but she never imagined how much passion she had for him. All her fantasies came together in one glorious fairy tale moment and Jennifer had found her prince after all.

The morning brought heavy rains making the roads treacherous and slippery so Jennifer was glad she allowed herself extra time to get to the bus station before the conditions worsened.

"What's taking so long?" she kept repeating to herself while waiting for Brian to arrive. Every time she looked at the oversized round clock on the bus station wall, it seemed time stood still. Jennifer couldn't wait sitting down any longer and walked over to the ticket booth while sirens blared in the background. As she turned to look out the pane glass window, one ambulance sped by and then another, and within seconds, yet another passed.

"Must have been one heck of an accident," said ole man Charlie at the ticket booth as Jennifer approached him. Charlie, now in his late sixties, had worked at the bus station for over twenty years and had seen it all. Watching Jennifer earlier sitting in the waiting area with her legs anxiously bobbing up and down and her hands clasped together between her knees, Charlie knew she must be waiting for someone special in her life.

"Excuse me sir," Jennifer began. "Do you have any idea when the 732 from Knoxville will arrive? You see I'm waiting for my Brian."

"Ma'am, I wish I knew. With the roads this slippery, I'm sure the buses are traveling a little slower and with all the accidents this morning, some roads might even be blocked. I'm sure he'll be turning that corner any moment."

Before Charlie could go on, a stern voice came over the speaker system. "This is Captain Miller, will all employees please report to the back meeting room," the loud speaker shrieked. "I repeat, will all employees please report to the back meeting room immediately. We have a Code Red."

"What in the world is that?" Jennifer mumbled to herself. In his twenty years of working at the station, this was only the second time Charlie heard this code being used. He quickly jumped off his stool and excused himself, but not before placing a closed sign at the ticket booth.

"Oh this is just great," Jennifer said sarcastically to herself. "I need information and now everyone is in the backroom with a Code Red."

After what seemed like an eternity, the ticket agents and other employees came out from the backroom where they held an impromptu emergency meeting. Looking somber and flustered, they scrambled back to their positions and removed the closed signs they had posted.

"Charlie, please," Jennifer pleaded, her voice trembling now. "Can you tell me when the 732 is arriving?"

After clearing his throat a couple of times Charlie responded, "I'm sorry to be the one to tell you this, young lady, but there seems to have been an accident involving the bus from Knoxville...they are taking the injured and the...well..., the passengers to West Mount Hospital."

Stunned, Jennifer stared at Charlie's gloomy face in disbelief, unable to utter a word.

"Ma'am, are you all right?" Charlie asked, not receiving any response. "Would you like a glass of water or something?"

Jennifer turned around and never answered as she hurriedly headed to her car in the parking lot. She prayed Brian would be all right, sitting there at the hospital waiting for her with that big beautiful smile of his, and they would embrace, and she would never let him out of her sight again. She didn't realize how much she missed his smell, his laughter, and his strong arms wrapped around her.

The drive to the hospital was a blur, but Jennifer snapped back to reality upon arriving at the emergency room to utter chaos.

"Miss, excuse me, miss?" Jennifer asked, hopelessly trying to get the attention of a nurse while people bumped into her from different directions. She finally flagged down an intern who was rushing towards the emergency room doors.

"Excuse me sir, where can I find the bus passengers from Knoxville?" Jennifer asked as she struggled to keep pace with him.

"They're all over miss," blurted the intern as he began to sprint towards another ambulance. "The injured are in the emergency room; the ones that have passed are being moved to the morgue; and the ones that weren't seriously hurt are in the lobby around the corner and down the hall."

"The ones that have passed are being moved to the morgue?" Jennifer repeated to herself. She hadn't even thought of the possibility that some of the passengers could be dead. Andrew Stone, a local newspaper reporter, was assigned to cover the breaking story and stopped to ask Jennifer if she was one of the passengers from the bus crash.

"No I'm not sir, but do you know where I could find someone who was on the bus?" she asked in return.

"I heard a supervisor has a list of the people that have come in from the crash site and the status of their condition," Andrew stated. "Let me take you there, miss. It's just around the corner in the lobby area." Andrew, holding his reporter notebook in one hand, took Jennifer by the arm and led her to the lobby as she trembled with fear.

It was difficult reaching the tall man in a white uniform who held the clipboard with the list of passengers, but after some pushing and shoving, Andrew managed to get Jennifer to the front of the crowd and she yelled out, "Brian Taylor!"

"Taylor, Brian Taylor," the man with the clipboard repeated to himself as he scoured the names on the paper using his pencil for guidance.

"Miss, you're going to have to go to the conference room just down the hallway to the left in order to get more information on his condition," stated the man. Andrew accompanied Jennifer as she walked to the conference room and inside, stood an elderly lady, a nurse, a young woman, and a clergy.

"Excuse me, but I was told to come here to get more information on Brian Taylor," said Jennifer. "I'm his girlfriend, and he was on the bus that was in that terrible accident. Can you please tell me where I could find him? I'm sure he's waiting for me to take him home."

The elderly lady walked gingerly over to Jennifer and pulled her aside introducing herself as a counselor for patient services. Reaching out to hold Jennifer's hands in hers, she said in a gentle, compassionate way, "I'm very sorry miss and I don't know how to tell you this, but unfortunately, Brian's injuries were too severe and he passed away in the ambulance on the way to the hospital. There wasn't anything that could be done for him. I'm so sorry."

Andrew grabbed Jennifer just in time, as her knees buckled and she fainted. He gently laid her down on the couch as the people in the room rushed to help. The nurse pulled out smelling salts from her pocket and tried feverishly to wake her. When she woke up and realized what she had just heard, Jennifer became inconsolable and began screaming. Andrew sat by her side and held her tightly as she cried, tears soaking through his shirt.

It was several hours before Jennifer was allowed to go see Brian to officially identify him. At her insistence, the reporter accompanied her into the morgue and Jennifer shivered as she entered the pale sterile room that contained several covered stretchers. As the doctor lifted up the white sheet draped over a lifeless body, Jennifer held her breath hoping there was some mistake and they had the wrong person. She gasped, instantly recognizing the man with blond curls and sweet lips lying on the gurney. It was true...Brian was gone. Jennifer reached towards his motionless body, and held his hand, while gently kissing his lips. With her body now slumped over on top of his, she asked out loud, "How could you possibly be gone? How could God have taken you from me? How could this have happened? I don't understand. Andrew, please wake him up."

Andrew gently rubbed Jennifer's back and said to her, "I'm so sorry for your loss Jennifer. I wish to God I could bring him back for you. I'm so very sorry. When you're ready, I'll make sure you get home."

"My sweet, sweet Brian," Jennifer whispered to him as her tears rolled down onto his face. "You'll always be my one true love, my sweet angel. You are with God now."

With one last kiss on his lips, Jennifer slowly left the room with Andrew and headed back to the conference room. Shortly after the police notified Brian's family by telephone of his death, and getting their approval to provide Jennifer with Brian's belongings, the desk clerk at the hospital gave her a small white plastic bag with Brian's possessions.

Andrew took her back home to her apartment and after finding out from Jennifer who her close friends were in town, Andrew telephoned Christie and Johanna who rushed right over. Once the ladies were inside the apartment and by Jennifer's side, an emotional Andrew returned to the hospital to finish his newspaper assignment.

The next day, Jennifer took the plastic bag to the park where she had planned to surprise him with a romantic afternoon picnic. As she sat on the blanket at the park, Jennifer looked down and realized that all she had left of Brian was now in this little bag which she opened for the first time. The bag contained a keychain, a wallet, a ticket stub, a small box, some loose sticks of gum, and a folded wrinkled piece of notebook paper. With tears streaming down her face, she unfolded the paper, reading it in a low whisper to herself.

"My dear Jennifer, you are the love of my life. Every breath I take, every second of the day, it is you that I long for. To hold you in my arms every day and never let you go. You are already in my heart, and now I want you by my side in life. I want to spend the rest of my life with you my sweetheart. Jennifer, will you do me the great honor of marrying me?"

Jennifer reached towards her heart with her trembling hands and looked towards the sky. She realized Brian had written down his engagement proposal to rehearse it on the bus while he traveled to Atlanta to meet her. Jennifer retrieved the small box from the baggie with Brian's possessions and slowly opened it. Inside was the most beautiful diamond ring she'd ever seen. As she slipped it on her finger, the ring fit as perfect as the red ruby shoes fit Dorothy in the Wizard of Oz.

Jennifer reached down deep in her front coat pocket and took out a paper. On it were the test results that she was going to surprise him with.

"You would have been such a good father, my love."

23 | Mother's Day 1964

*"Being a mother is learning about strengths you didn't
know you had, and dealing with fears you
didn't know existed." ~Linda Wooten*

Dear Summer,

You'll be eighteen soon and I wish you could read all the letters I've written to you every year so you know how much I've cared about you. I have them all here for you my sweetheart. I can't turn back the clock, but I want you to know that I think about you every single day. No matter how busy I am, you are always with me in my heart.

I wonder if you're going to get married and become a housewife, or do you plan on attending college instead? You know you can do both, don't you? It's a bit more challenging, but nothing and no one can ever stand in your way if you really want something badly enough. Did you ever become the singer I thought you would?

I think about your wedding day and you starting a family of your own. I'm so sorry I won't be there to watch and help you as you pick out that perfect dress to marry the man of your dreams. The only thing I can wish for is that you find a good young man, like your birth father, who will honor and cherish you like you deserve.

Summer, take your time with this. It is so important to meet the right person who you will hopefully be spending the rest of your life with. I had planned to do that with Michael, but my life took a different turn. Although I never married, I don't regret one moment of how my life turned out. I was blessed with you and with all my adoptive children.

Do you know that I still place an extra plate at the supper table for you? I tell the children it's just in case someone knocks on the door, so we'll be ready to invite them in and have them join us, but it's really for you, my sweetheart. Not a day goes by that you're not in my thoughts. You are as much a part of this family as the children are.

I love you my darling,

Your Mommy

24 | Coming Home

Jennifer flew back home, accompanying Brian's body to meet with his family and hers. She was distraught on the flight as her memories of Brian replayed in her mind like a movie being shown in slow motion. She tried desperately to rewrite the script in her head, hoping the outcome would change and Brian would still be alive, but flashbacks of Brian lying on the gurney in the cold sterile morgue kept freezing the movie frames.

The flight arrived on time and Jennifer's mother Katherine was waiting for her along with her oldest brother Benjamin III, and Cameron, the youngest of the boys, along with Brian's mother and his three brothers. Devon was away at law school and promised to call Jennifer as soon as she had settled down.

As Jennifer entered the airport lobby, she saw Brian's mother and his brothers first who were there to meet her and escort the casket to the funeral home. It was a tearful reunion as she paid her respects to the Taylor family and then she spotted her mother Katherine and her brothers.

"Mom!" she called out as she ran towards her family who was anxiously waiting for her.

"My dear child, it's so good to have you back home with us," replied Katherine with the boys repeating the same sentiment. "We're so sorry about Brian."

Jennifer wrapped her arms around all three of them and burst into tears. The ride home was solemn and as soon as they arrived, Jennifer asked the family to gather in the main room.

"Mom, I don't know what I'm going to do. I feel so lost. My Brian is gone. You should have seen him at the hospital. He looked so peaceful."

"Honey, Brian loved you very much, and now he is in God's arms. You have to believe that."

"Jen," Cameron sheepishly began to speak. "I don't know exactly what to say, but I want you to know that we're all here for you, and I hope you stay for a while. I really miss you."

"Cam, I miss you too. You're so sweet for saying that. And Ben, I miss our talks...I miss all of you. If only Daddy were here."

Jennifer's father, Benjamin, passed away unexpectedly when she was a junior in high school and it had been a devastating blow to the entire family. He had the same congenital heart defect like the one that suddenly killed his own father when Benjamin was only a youngster. Deep down, Benjamin always felt, he too, would die young. His passion with the element of time was the result of a constant sensation that time was always literally ticking away.

After Brian's funeral, several days went by before Jennifer could muster enough strength to leave the house. The morning sickness was getting worse, and her family was beginning to suspect something was wrong besides the normal grieving process, so Jennifer knew she would have to break the news soon that she was carrying Brian's baby.

She began taking a stroll in the mornings in order to clear her thoughts and sort out the options that were confronting her. Although she missed her girlfriends terribly, school seemed a world away, and now, she had to deal with potentially being a single mother.

"This wasn't the way my life was supposed to turn out," Jennifer would say to herself. She had envisioned marrying Brian, having their baby, finishing school and starting a design company.

"Jen, can I walk with you today?" Katherine asked hoping her daughter would welcome her companionship both as a mother and a friend.

"Sure Mom. I would love that. Isn't it beautiful out here today?"

"You've come back at the best time of the year Jen."

"Mom, there's something I need to tell you, and I don't know where to begin."

"Take a deep breath, sweetheart, and just start at the beginning. You'll see how the words will come to you. What is it, darling? Is it Brian?"

"Well, in a way, yes," Jennifer responded, trying to organize her next words. With her gaze fixed to the ground, she took long strides along the walkway, cupping her hands together. Halfway through the garden area, she stopped and turned to her mother.

"Mom, I'm pregnant."

Katherine didn't expect to hear those words. A million thoughts bombarded her mind, and it took several seconds before she realized there was utter silence.

"Mom, are you all right?"

"Why yes, honey. It's just that I'm a little stunned." With all the grieving, it seemed disloyal to Katherine to have a happy moment, although she was thrilled at the thought of becoming a grandmother.

"My poor girl, you've been keeping this to yourself all this time. Why didn't you say something sooner?"

"Mom, I'm so lost. I don't know what I'm going to do."

"What do you mean by that, honey? You are going to keep this baby, aren't you? Oh, Jen, please say you are."

"Honestly, I don't know, Mom. I'm very confused. I need some time to think this through."

"I understand, honey. You've been through a lot in a very short period of time. Please think about this carefully, and if you need to talk to someone, you know you can speak with the pastor at St. Brendan's Parish. He's known you your entire life and he deeply cares for you, as if you were his own child. Promise me you'll think about it. Promise me Jen."

"All right, Mom, I promise. I'll ask him if I can come to the church on Wednesday morning and speak with him, but this will have to be my own decision."

Katherine stayed up all night tormented with the secret she'd been keeping from Jennifer her entire life. She realized the time had come to tell her, and although Katherine knew that one day the truth would be told, the time had never seemed right before. Katherine worried that in Jennifer's fragile state of mind, telling her now might push her into further turmoil and may even cause a miscarriage.

The following morning Katherine telephoned the pastor to ask for his help and guidance with Jennifer. Since Benjamin passed away, he had become Katherine's loyal confidant and source of support in addition to her children. Katherine recently began doing more charity work at the church to keep busy since the children now had their own lives and she organized small fundraisers to help the local orphanage.

This time, she once again leaned on the Pastor for his advice. He had never let her down before, so it was no surprise when he offered to be the one to tell Jennifer. The Pastor knew the situation well, and if someone was going to tell Jennifer the family secret, Katherine wanted it to be him.

25 | Letters To The Children

"I want adoption to be part of my child's story,
but I don't want it to be his/her only story."
~ Jennifer Ann Holt

Throughout the years, Chaya received letters from each of the birth mothers every Mother's Day. Heather always sent two letters, one for Rose and one for Chaya. She never forgot Chaya's generosity, and although she eventually married and had two more children, Rose was special in her heart.

Heather always asked for photographs of the daughter she adored, but could not keep, and she always asked for information on her progress. Although Chaya invited Heather to visit every year, she never came back to the home where she gave birth to Rose, too afraid of disrupting her environment and confusing the child. Although it was very hard on Heather, she was content knowing Rose was happy and taken care of.

Eve on the other hand, worked up the courage to visit Alexander when he turned two and then sporadically throughout the years. Although it was difficult at first, Eve realized her son was also an innocent victim of her uncle's attack, and she was proud he had flourished despite his deafness.

She learned some sign language in order to be able to better communicate with her son, but just seeing him running around and interacting with his siblings brought her immense joy. Eve would say that Alex turned out to be "just perfect" and she was glad at the decision she made to place him with Chaya and give him the loving home he deserved.

Introducing herself as Chaya's friend at first, Patricia would stop by every couple of years to visit with her son Kendrick. During her visits, she played with him for hours and was able to get to come to know her child. Kendrick was always happy to see the lady with the black skin just like his and Teddy's. Since he was a small child, Kendrick called her Pisha instead of Patricia, since he couldn't pronounce her full name. Their bond continued to grow throughout Kendrick's life and he was proud to say he had two fathers and two mothers.

The letters arrived every year carrying heartfelt sentiments, stories, dreams and more importantly, answers to the future questions these children were bound to ask. The one thing that was consistent in the letters was the love that these birth mothers had for their children and their welfare, and they were all grateful Chaya provided them with the opportunity and the support they needed in order to give their children a chance at life. It was important to the mothers to relay that message and to Chaya's surprise, most of the mothers were open to meeting their children in the future if that's what the children wanted.

26 | The Family Secret

Jennifer arrived a little early for the conference with her pastor, so she wandered into the gardens to wait for him to arrive. She found comfort among the white and pink dogwoods and azaleas. The nuns tended to the grounds around the church premises, and the foliage was blooming with life. The beauty of the gardens conveyed timeless love and nurturing, and it was obvious a lot of care and attention was given to them.

Quaint sitting areas were nestled throughout the grounds with small angelic cherub statues scattered strategically where the cobble stone trails meandered. It was a peaceful ambiance and the Pastor held many personal conferences there while strolling along its paths.

"Hello, Jennifer, it's so good to see you again," the Pastor said as he walked towards Jennifer with outstretched arms.

"Good morning, Pastor," replied Jennifer with a cordial smile. It had been many years since she had spoken to him, so she was a bit reserved with her greeting.

"Mother advised me to meet with you regarding a very personal matter. Do you mind very much if we take a walk through the gardens while we talk?"

"Of course not, let's walk along this path," the Pastor gestured to Jennifer with his arm pointing the way. "God listens to you not only in church, but even out here on these grounds. What's better than to be among the beautiful plants and flowers he so graciously blesses us with? But first let me offer you my most deep-felt condolences for the loss of Brian. From what I've been told, he was such a good, decent young man. Always put his family first. That was indeed a very terrible tragedy."

"Thank you for those kind words, Pastor. I guess that's partly why I'm here, but not in the way you might think."

"Go on, my child."

"When Brian told me he'd planned to visit me at the Art Institute, I had some really big news I recently found out about. I figured the news would be a shock to him, and I didn't know if he would be excited about it, but I was hoping he would be."

"Go on."

"There's no easy way to say this, especially to you, since you're a pastor and all, so I'm going to just say it. I'm pregnant with Brian's baby, and now I'm not so sure I want to keep it." The Pastor looked at her with a reassuring face, letting her continue her story. "I know that sounds terrible, but I don't know if I can raise a child alone. Mother is very supportive, but she's not always going to be around, and I want to be able to finish school and start a business. I know that may sound harsh, but without Brian helping me to raise this baby, I don't know if I have the strength to do this on my own."

The Pastor collected his thoughts and asked for guidance from the Lord above in choosing the right words to say to Jennifer. He knew what he was about to tell her could impact her decision.

"My dear child, nobody can guarantee what the future is going to hold for us. You just experienced that with the unexpected loss of Brian, but one thing we do know right this moment, is that you are carrying a life inside of you that was formed and created out of a union of love."

The Pastor asked Jennifer to sit down on the bench right next to where they were standing and took her hands into his. Although he was used to relaying both good, as well as unfortunate news to his parishioners, it was never easy and he always asked the Lord for guidance in choosing the right comforting words.

"You're going to have to trust me Jennifer. Your mother came to me the other day in anguish. Katherine wanted to tell you something, but she wasn't sure how you'd react, so she wanted me to speak with you."

"What is it, Pastor? Please tell me."

"Please listen to me carefully with an open heart."

"You're scaring me, Pastor."

"I don't mean to, Jennifer, but this is very important, and your mother believes it's time you knew."

"Time I knew what?"

"Jennifer, your father Benjamin, and your mother Katherine, came to me a long time ago with a longing. They had the three boys and life was pleasant, but both your parents longed passionately for a daughter. When Katherine found out she couldn't have any more children after Cameron was born, she was devastated."

"What are you telling me, Pastor?"

"What I'm trying to tell you Jennifer, is that they longed so much for a daughter, they wanted me to help them find a baby girl that they could adopt and raise as their own."

"Oh my God!" Jennifer gasped as she tried desperately to search for words.

"I know this is a lot to take in right now, Jennifer, and in your condition, I beg you to take a moment to gather your thoughts."

"Oh my God! My mother and father are not really my parents, and my brothers aren't even my real brothers? How could they keep this from me all these years? How could they?"

"Jennifer, you couldn't have asked for two people to love you more and you know that deep in your heart."

Jennifer burst into tears as the Pastor placed his arm gently around her shoulders. "Jennifer, listen to me for a moment. Your parents have loved you and raised you as their own daughter. Your father, Benjamin, adored you. Ever since he first laid eyes on you, you wrapped a string of lights around his heart. You were his little girl and your Mother beamed with joy when she brought you home. Your brothers were thrilled with their new baby sister. I remember Jonathon wanted to name you Little Angel because that's who you reminded him of. After a little prodding, Jonathon finally agreed to name you, Jennifer, only because it started with the same first letter as his name."

Jennifer revealed a smile at the story because she could picture Jonathon, who always wanted to have his way, finally agreeing to the name.

"Jennifer, I know this is a shock to you right now, but don't think of your family as anything but your family. You are an Alden through and through, and you will always be."

"Do the boys know about this?"

"No, your brothers were young when you arrived into their home and they were simply told they had a little sister that was going to be a part of the family. Katherine told them that God delivered you to them and they never questioned it. If you want to tell your brothers, she will support you. It's up to you. Your mother wants that to be your decision to make."

Endless questions were running through Jennifer's head. Who were her birth parents? What do they look like? Are they still alive? Does she have other brothers or sisters? Where did she come from? Why was she placed for adoption? She didn't know which one to ask first.

"Jennifer, I'm sure you must have a lot of questions, and I will do my best to answer them, but before I do, I want to let you know the reason that your mother wanted you to know the truth at this time in your life."

Jennifer was confused, but was listening intently to every word the Pastor was saying. "Your parents have always thanked the good Lord above that your birth mother chose to place you for adoption for they couldn't have pictured their life without you. Now you have that choice before you, Jennifer. It is your choice, but it's one that should not be taken lightly. Although your mother would like nothing more for you to raise this child, there are thousands of other families waiting for their prayers to be answered with the arrival of a baby."

"I know that, Pastor. I'm just very confused right now."

"That's understandable, Jennifer. If there is anything I can help you with please let me know. You are not alone, and we are all here to help you any way we can."

"Do you know who my parents were?" Jennifer asked, not certain if she wanted to know the answer just yet.

"Jennifer, what I can tell you, is that your birth mother loved you very much. She was a young girl, several years younger than you right now when she became pregnant. This was many years ago, and in those days, it was very difficult for a young girl in that situation. As wrong as that may seem now, many girls were compelled to leave town and place their baby up for adoption."

"Your birth mother made the right decision for herself at that time and she decided to give you a chance at a life with a good family. I was called by the director of the Home for Girls to help find a good family to raise you. A week prior to that, Ben and Katherine asked me to help them find them a baby girl to adopt. It was God's will to bring you both together."

"Can you tell me who my birth parents are?"

"Jennifer, adoption records are confidential, and the Home for Girls would not be at liberty to discuss that with you, but you can leave your name with them and if your birth parents are also searching for you and they contact the Home, they will try to reunite you all."

"Honestly, I don't know if I'm ready for that right now," Jennifer said, shaking her head. "I think I need a little time for myself. I need to sort this out."

"Jennifer, there's a home in Sparta that welcomes young ladies in your situation who are confused and need a little time to think things out. It's a beautiful ranch with wonderful gardens, and the woman who lives there has taken in many girls in distress. The last I heard, she was raising seven adopted children, and I'm sure she can use the help."

"Maybe the distraction is just what I need right now. Can you ask her if I could at least stop by to visit the ranch?"

"I have no doubt you would be very welcome there. I'll give you the directions and remember, I'm just a telephone call away."

"Thank you, Pastor John, for everything you've done for me and my family, and I'm glad you were the one to tell me. I'll be all right. I adore my family and it was you who brought us together."

"No my dear Jennifer. It was God."

27 | Self-Discovery

When Jennifer returned home after her meeting with Pastor John, her mother was nervously awaiting her. Katherine expected the worse, but was surprised when Jennifer entered their home, calm and collected.

"How are you Jennifer?" said Katherine in a low tone.

"Mother, I need a little time to digest what I just found out today from Pastor John," Jennifer replied. "So please give me some space, but I want you to know that I love you and daddy for adopting me and bringing me into this family, and I love my brothers too. You are my family and nothing will change that. I just need a little time to sort things out."

Within days, Jennifer had packed some clothes, bid a fond farewell to her family, and headed for Sparta, Tennessee. Katherine had discretely slipped a letter into the side pocket of her suitcase, hoping Jennifer would read it when she arrived and unpacked at the ranch she was heading to. The bus ride to Sparta allowed Jennifer time to reflect on the events of the last couple of months and what she recently learned from the Pastor. She foresaw a time in the future when she would seek her birth mother, but for now, she was content in knowing she was loved.

The taxi she took from the bus station left her at the ranch gate, and Jennifer slowly walked to the front door. With suitcase in hand, she took a deep breath and started walking up the porch steps toward the door. She paused and took a long look around at the large trees surrounding the grounds and in the distance, Jennifer could see an endless array of rolling hills covered in green terrain. Beautiful lush gardens lined the borders of the house, reminding her of the church gardens, and suddenly a feeling of peace and serenity enveloped her. She was anxious to meet this lady named Chaya, who seemed to have a special heart and love for the children she adopted.

The tranquility was quickly interrupted by two children who roared around the corner of the house squealing with laughter. Jack and Jacob were running to hide from Amanda in an afternoon game of hide and seek. They only had one minute to hide before Amanda stopped counting and began the search and as they hurried up the steps towards the house, they almost knocked Jennifer off her feet.

"Well hello there," said Jennifer, trying to steady herself.

"Sorry miss, we have to go," blurted Jacob as he and his brother ran into the house. "Mom, someone's out there on the porch," he yelled to Chaya as he darted upstairs to hide in a closet.

"Kids, slow down," Chaya responded to a now empty room. Before Jennifer had time to ring the doorbell, Chaya appeared at the front door.

"Uh, hello," mumbled a startled Jennifer. "I'm Jennifer Alden."

"Hello, I'm Chaya Rose. It's a pleasure to meet you."

"I see you have your hands full. Maybe I'll come back another time."

"Oh no please, come on in. By the looks of your suitcase, I'm sure you've come a long way."

"Well no, not really. I live just a couple of hours away, but I wasn't sure how long I'd be staying."

Chaya invited Jennifer inside and placed her suitcase in the corner of the foyer. She excused herself for a moment to check on the chicken that was baking in the oven and to get cold iced sweet tea for her guest. The day was unusually warm, and Jennifer was starting to feel the exhaustion of the trip. While Chaya was in the kitchen, Jennifer glanced around the large living and dining area, marveling at how tidy the house was kept considering seven children lived there. She smiled as Chaya walked into the room.

"How do you do it?" questioned an incredulous Jennifer. "How do you manage the ranch and raise all the children by yourself?"

"Oh, I have a lot of help," answered Chaya, as she handed her the glass of sweet tea and laid a plate of cookies on the coffee table. "Rose, my oldest, is a big help, and all the kids pitch in when they're not chasing each other around."

Jennifer laughed, having just barely escaped being run over by two of the children. "I know what you mean. My brothers and I were the same way growing up."

Jennifer paused, reflecting on a childhood memory when she was part of the Alden Three. The memory brought a smile to her face, and Jennifer blankly stared at the glass of tea she was holding.

"You seem to have something on your mind Jennifer. It is Jennifer, right?" Chaya confirmed hoping she had not forgotten her name.

"I have a lot on my mind and I feel a little embarrassed being here."

"Well I hope I can make you comfortable, because I don't want anyone to ever feel embarrassed in my home." There was a long pause as Jennifer gathered her thoughts and finally broke the silence.

"Miss Chaya, I've just been through a lot, and I needed to leave the town I come from and have some time to sort things out."

"Well you've come to the right place. You'll have the time, but I don't know if you'll have any peace and quiet."

"That's all right. Like I told the Pastor, I could use a little distraction."

Chaya didn't bother to ask if the Pastor she was referring to was the same Pastor John who mysteriously kept sending young girls in distress her way. "Tell me what's on your mind, Jennifer. I'm here to listen."

"Can we please go take a short walk?" Jennifer asked hoping she would say yes.

"Of course we can. Just give me a minute to turn down the temperature on the stove so supper doesn't burn and let me tell the kids where I'll be. You're in luck because I made enough for nine today. Something told me to throw some more chicken in the oven."

Jennifer laughed at Chaya's quick wit and felt very comfortable in her presence even though they just met. The house had a warm cozy feel, and she could sense an immense amount of love all around. As they started their walk, Jennifer searched to find a starting place to tell her story.

"Miss Chaya, I grew up in a very loving family. I adored my father, Benjamin, and my mother. My father passed away when I was in high school and that was a very difficult time for me since we were very close. I have three older brothers who always watched out for me and took care of me even when they preferred to go and play with the other boys."

"Anyway, I met Brian in high school, and we fell madly in love. I had dreams of being an artist and opening up a design company, so I enrolled at the Art Institute of Atlanta and left the town I grew up in, my family, and Brian. It had been nine weeks since I last saw Brian so he wanted to take a bus and come visit me for several days and see my new apartment. As you could imagine, I couldn't wait to see him, and although my girlfriends were a little envious that my boyfriend was coming, they were so happy for me."

Chaya listened carefully knowing that something must have gone terribly wrong. Her heart was already aching for Jennifer since she could sense Jennifer was in a lot of pain.

"The day Brian was to arrive, there was a terrible rainstorm and the roads were wet. For hours I waited for him at the bus station, but the bus never arrived. It veered off the road at a slippery curve, and Brian was severely injured. He died in the ambulance on the way to the hospital."

"I'm so sorry, Jennifer. You poor girl."

Jennifer quickly continued her story so she wouldn't lose her train of thought. "After I identified his body, they gave me all his belongings. All I had left of him was in a small plastic hospital bag."

"The next day I went to the park where I was planning on surprising him with an outdoor picnic. I sat on the blanket I was going to use for our outing and opened the bag they gave me at the hospital with his possessions. Besides his wallet, keys, and some gum, there was a little box with a ring in it and a crumpled note."

Jennifer stopped and burst into tears, because the memory was too vivid and hard to relive. Chaya reached out and gave her a warm embrace, trying to soothe her pain. After a couple of minutes, Jennifer continued her story.

"Brian had written the words down so he could memorize his marriage proposal to me during his bus ride."

"Jennifer, I am truly so sorry. What you must have gone through."

"The sad part is, Miss Chaya, I was going to tell him I was pregnant with his child and I never got the chance." Chaya took a deep breath. Thoughts of Michael raced through her mind since she never told him either, and even though much time had passed, it was a difficult secret to live with.

"After Brian's funeral, I told my mother I was pregnant and that I didn't know if I wanted to keep the baby and raise it as a single mom. She made me promise not to make any rash decisions and asked me to go see Pastor John."

It had to be the same Pastor John, Chaya thought to herself. One day she would have to seek him out.

"Miss Chaya, my mother had spoken to the Pastor and asked him to be the one to tell me the big family secret." Chaya was intrigued, but patiently waited for Jennifer to continue. "He told me how my parents wanted so desperately to have a daughter after they had three sons and how my mother was unable to conceive again. They asked the Pastor to help them find a baby girl they could call their own. After all these years, can you believe I just found out I'm adopted?" Chaya stared in disbelief as Jennifer continued. "The revelation is finally sinking in, and I know my family adores me, but I needed to get away to think about what I'm going to do about my baby. That's why

I'm here. Do you understand?"

Chaya sat in silence for she understood all too well. There was a compassion and sweetness about Jennifer that made Chaya feel she could confide in her. She had never spoken before about Summer to any of the other girls that came to the ranch. This time however it felt right, and she hoped Jennifer would understand why a mother might make the choice to give up her child even when she doesn't want to.

Chaya motioned to Jennifer to come closer. "Let's sit down on this bench and let me tell you a little story about me that may help you dear. When I was sixteen, I met the boy that I thought I would spend the rest of my life with. His name was Michael, and we were madly in love and wanted to get married. One day, he went to speak to my father to let him know his intentions to marry me and to seek his blessing with our union. Well, my father wanted nothing to do with Michael and told him we were too young for marriage."

"I was waiting for him at our favorite lake for him to return from my parent's house with what I thought would be good news. Needless to say, we were both devastated at my father response, but Michael and I decided to say our vows to each other and marry ourselves under the eyes of God."

Jennifer was on the edge of her seat, listening to every word Chaya was saying. "We were silly young kids back then, thinking everything was going to be just fine. Our 'marriage' would be our little secret, and when we were old enough under the law, we would elope and make it official. We decided to consummate our marriage on that very day, and every chance we could, we would meet up at the lake and be with each other."

Chaya paused for a minute to gather her thoughts since she never had told the story before. It was emotional for her, but she knew it would be important that Jennifer hear it.

"Are you okay, Miss Chaya?" Jennifer asked with concern.

"Yes, my dear, I just need a moment."

"You don't have to go on if you don't want to," Jennifer said, knowing how hard this must be for her.

"Let me go on. I became ill and began throwing up, so my mother took me to the doctor where we learned that I was pregnant. Back in my day, this brought shame on my family and my father would have none of it and demanded I place my baby up for adoption."

Chaya clasped her hands and looked down, shaking her head in silence. "Jennifer, that baby I had growing inside of me was one that Michael and I created together in a moment of complete passion and love. I begged my father to let me keep the baby, but he insisted it would have brought shame to the family name."

"Although I was devastated, I reluctantly agreed and my father found a girls home where I lived during the last months of my pregnancy so no one in our town would know. I gave birth to a baby girl that I never even got to hold in my arms. The nurses whisked her away so I wouldn't become attached and change my mind."

"I don't know what to say, Miss Chaya," Jennifer responded, with her heart aching.

"My one regret is that I never told Michael a thing. He never knew why I left town and why I stopped seeing him. It was just too hard for me. He was a father and he never knew."

Tears came down Chaya's face and she quickly wiped them away. "Jennifer, I wanted to tell you this because you have a very important choice to make that can change your entire life. The children you see running around here are my precious angels, and I have comfort knowing my baby was adopted by a family who so desperately wanted a child like I did. My dear, you are here because of the same reason. And look at all the joy and love you brought to your own family."

Hearing Chaya's story brought comfort to Jennifer and she now realized why Chaya helped so many lost souls, and why she was determined to be a good mother. If the mothers of her children didn't have a place to go and be taken care of, who knows where their babies would be now, and Jennifer realized that the two beautiful lively children who almost ran her over on the porch earlier are here because of Chaya and her loving heart.

"Jennifer, I've never told anyone my story until today, and I hope it will make a difference in your life. Whatever you decide, it is your choice, but remember, that you can raise your child even if you are single mother. It might not be easy, but I have no doubt you will be a wonderful mother, or if you choose, you can give hope to a family and place your baby for adoption."

Jennifer hugged Chaya and thanked her for listening and telling her story. They walked silently back to the house, each lost in their own thoughts. After supper, Jennifer settled in the guest room, and for the first time in a long while, she slept peacefully and soundly. Chaya invited her to stay for as long as she needed.

28 | Part Of The Family

"The bond that links your true family is not one of blood,
but of respect and joy in each other's life."
~ Richard Bach

Knowing Jennifer was exhausted both mentally and physically, Chaya let her sleep the following morning until she was ready to awaken on her own. She was making early preparations for the evening supper meal when Jennifer walked into the kitchen around mid-morning.

"Good morning, young lady, rise and shine," Chaya greeted Jennifer who was still wiping her eyes, trying to get them to stay open.

"Good morning, Miss Chaya. Can I help you with that?"

"Why don't you run back up and change your night gown into something you don't need to keep clean, and I'll show you around the ranch, because I could definitely use the help."

Growing up in town, Jennifer never experienced life on a farm, but she was about to receive her first lesson. After breakfast and a quick tour of the ranch and grounds, Jennifer began her day learning to prepare the feed for the two cows in the pasture, Hickory and Chicory.

Jennifer was impressed at the sheer size of the two cows and as she got near them, Hickory swung her tail over to swat a fly and smacked Jennifer on the side of her face. Startled, Jennifer let out a shriek, and Chaya burst out laughing. Day by day, she took on more chores around the ranch and really began to enjoy the time she spent with the cows and looking after them. As it turned out, the farm life was therapeutic for Jennifer and she especially enjoyed it when the children were around.

When Rose met Jennifer who was four years older, she instantly took a liking to her, because it was like having the big sister she never had. Alex, being an artist like Jennifer, was fascinated by the charcoal drawings she did of the flower gardens that surrounded the house and as time went by, Jennifer began teaching Alex the different techniques she used, mixing charcoals with pastel colors to bring out the vibrancy of the flowers. He had never tried his hand at sketching on drawing paper with different mediums before, and was quite surprised that he was talented at it.

In the evening after supper, the children gathered in the large living room to talk or just relax, while Chaya read stories to the youngest ones. Jennifer and Alex took this opportunity to sketch the family while the others were distracted, listening to Chaya reading. With only the glow of the evening table lamps, their drawings captured dramatic lighting effects of all the different postures the family displayed.

Alex drew the twins lying on their bellies, both with their hands to their chins and their legs criss-crossed behind them, as they listened to one of their favorite stories being read. Jennifer sketched Sarah nestled on Chaya's lap with Amanda sitting beside her, her head on Chaya's shoulder. Kendrick, whose fascination with architecture was growing, was usually portrayed with a tool in his hand constructing a project on the work table along the west side of the living room.

Rose, who was now a developing young teenager, sat by Jennifer as she sketched and spoke to her about clothes and boys. Jennifer was a good listener, but she was careful to avoid giving any parental advice she thought should come from Chaya.

Another couple of months passed before Jennifer began to show her pregnancy. Although they had not spoken about the ultimate decision Jennifer was going to have to make, Chaya secretly hoped Jennifer would decide to keep the baby, for she was wonderful with her own children. Chaya was a little concerned how her family would feel once Jennifer had the baby and went back home to continue living her life. It was the first time that one of the girls lived with the family for so many months, and Jennifer was definitely going to be missed. She was a special soul and Chaya and the children had grown extremely fond of her.

As Jennifer's belly grew larger, Chaya wanted her to rest and not worry about feeding the cows, which she really enjoyed, or even helping around the house, but Jennifer insisted on doing the lighter chores. In the evening, she began reading to the children along with Chaya and they started creating their own stories and alternating between characters. The children got a big kick out of this and before long, they were all entertaining each other with role playing and storytelling.

As Chaya and Jennifer's friendship grew closer, they enjoyed many afternoon strolls around the gardens, and one day, Jennifer surprised Chaya on their walk with a question she wasn't expecting.

"Miss Chaya, can I ask you something?" Jennifer began not knowing how to ask her question.

"Of course, my dear. You can ask me absolutely anything."

"Do you really think I can raise this baby by myself? I mean, do you think it's right if I raise an only child being one parent? I mean, I grew up with three brothers, and your children are being raised together with seven brothers and sisters. Don't you think my baby will be too lonely?"

Chaya was trying to figure out what Jennifer was really trying to say before she responded. "Jennifer, I was an only child, and yes it was lonely at times, but who's to say you won't have more children in the future. You have a wonderful family waiting for you back home who you even said will welcome this child with open arms."

Chaya was carefully studying her expression before Jennifer continued. "I guess what I'm really asking is, can I stay here for a little while after the baby is born? I'll help you with everything and with the children too."

Chaya was taken aback by the question. "Of course you can stay with us my dear child and I was hoping you would. You can stay as long as you wish."

Tears began to flow down Jennifer's flushed cheeks and a huge sigh of relief overcame her as she took a long deep breath. She couldn't bear the thought of leaving the children, especially with them looking forward to holding the new baby. What's more, she hoped Chaya would teach her how to be a good mother. "You won't regret it, Miss Chaya. I promise you."

Jennifer reached over and hugged Chaya as tightly as her belly permitted. It was just a matter of weeks before Jennifer was due to give birth. She had gained some weight in the last month as her body prepared the womb for the baby's arrival.

Chaya couldn't wait to see this new life come into the world, and she was thrilled she had been a part of Jennifer's decision to keep the child and raise it herself. For months, Jennifer read different books she checked out from the local library on giving birth, and decided she wanted a natural home birth. A midwife had already been chosen and was waiting to be called when the time arrived.

All the kids had been secretly preparing for the baby's arrival and they made their own gifts to welcome the baby. One evening, Chaya rounded up the entire family to surprise Jennifer with presents for her and the baby. Kendrick built a beautiful wooden cradle that was attached to two arched arms protruding from the two pillars that towered from the floor, allowing the crib to gently rock back and forth. It was his own design, and it took him over five weeks to build it in the barn with Teddy's guidance. Jennifer was stunned and speechless when Kendrick unveiled the cradle and it was the most beautiful crib she had ever seen.

Alex gave Jennifer a pastel sketch he secretly drew of her in the garden, capturing a quiet moment when she was sitting on the lawn caressing her belly under a cool shady tree. She had been sitting with her eyes closed, her back against the tree trunk, singing softly to the unborn child she carried.

Little did Alex know that Jennifer was also speaking to the baby's father, Brian, at the exact time he was drawing her. In her heart, Jennifer felt Brian was watching over her and their unborn child, and she ached for him. When Alex gave her the drawing, Jennifer burst with tears of joy, because she remembered that day out in the garden, and it meant the world to her to have it forever captured in a drawing so tenderly as Alex did.

Amanda, Jack and Jordon packed two boxes with some of their baby clothes they had worn as infants to give to Jennifer as a present, digging through the chest full of hand-me-downs Chaya collected over the years to give to the new mothers. Not knowing what sex the baby was going to be, the three children opened the chest and carefully chose their favorite outfits, filling one box with pink clothes and one with blue.

Amanda collected a varied selection of toys she thought the baby would enjoy and Sarah brought some flowers she had picked herself from the garden and had Chaya put them in a vase for her. Rose waited patiently as all her brothers and sisters gave their gifts to Jennifer and when it was her turn, she brought out a beautiful tan leather-bound journal and held it in her outstretched hands.

"Jennifer, I would like for you to have this," Rose said as Jennifer reached out to receive the journal.

"It's beautiful, Rose."

Rose continued, "For the last seven months, you have been an inspiration and a true friend to me. You have listened to all my craziness and helped me try to figure out boys, homework and even life. I wanted your baby to know what a beautiful person you are and what you have meant to me, so I have been keeping a diary of everything we have done and shared together. I also wanted the baby to know how much you loved it before it was born and how much you're looking forward to meeting it. Now, I want you to have this journal so you can continue writing in it. It is my present to you and the baby."

Jennifer was truly overwhelmed and again was moved to tears. "I will treasure this, Rose, and I will continue to write where you left off. One day my baby will read this and know what a wonderful friend you have been to me too."

Rose was an exceptionally sweet and profound young woman, and Chaya was so proud of her. The evening ended with many hugs, tears and much laughter around the living room where they gathered every evening.

29 | A Mother's Intuition

*"We must let go of the life we have planned, so as to
accept the one that is waiting for us."*
~ Joseph Campbell

Several days had passed since the children showered
Jennifer with baby gifts when she began to feel the pangs of
labor. Although her baby was not due for another couple of
weeks, her water broke as she struggled to get out of bed in the
morning. Chaya had prepared her for that moment, so although
she was scared, Jennifer kept her composure as she walked
towards the bedroom door.

As she reached for the doorknob, a stabbing pain in the
back of her head caused her to fall to the ground. Jennifer began
sweating profusely and the pain was making her gasp for air as
she reached to grab a hold of the door. Although she tried to
scream for help, her muffled sounds were barely audible.
Jennifer lay helpless on the bedroom floor while Chaya was
downstairs with Rose preparing breakfast.

As Chaya turned to place a large plate of scrambled eggs
on the table, it slipped from her hands, crashing to the ground,
breaking into bits and pieces. She stared at the pieces of the

broken plate scattered throughout the kitchen floor, when an awful feeling came over her.

"Something's wrong!" she said to herself as she made her way up the stairway towards Jennifer's room. "Something is terribly wrong!"

Seeing her mother race out of the kitchen, and run up the stairs, Rose followed suit right behind her.

"Jennifer!" she screamed as she hurriedly knocked on the door. Before she could wait for an answer, Chaya opened the door and found Jennifer unconscious and barely breathing.

"Oh my God!" screamed Rose as she saw Chaya kneeling over and breathing into Jennifer's mouth.

"Rose, call an ambulance and call Dr. Overton, hurry!" gasped Chaya in between breaths as she pumped on Jennifer's chest.

"Jen, don't do this to us now. You've got to live. Your baby needs you. Come on, breathe honey. Come on breathe."

Rose called for an ambulance and also summoned their family physician, Dr. Overton, who lived two ranches down the valley. She told him they had an emergency and he rushed over as fast as he could. Although retired for fifteen years, Dr. Overton always responded when needed since he lived in Sparta all his life, and knew its people well.

When the doctor arrived, he found Chaya kneeling over Jennifer giving her mouth to mouth resuscitation and chest compressions. She had managed to keep Jennifer breathing and when the doctor entered the room, he quickly took over.

After what seemed like an eternity, an ambulance finally arrived at the ranch, but by this time, Jennifer's breathing had stopped. The rescue personnel instructed Chaya to leave the room so they could work on Jennifer. The children were downstairs, hysterical and crying when Chaya reached them.

"All we can do now is pray," Chaya told the children as she gathered them around her while trying to catch her own breath. "Jen and the baby are in God's hands."

The seconds turned into minutes as everyone paced back and forth in the downstairs living room that had been the center of so many memorable moments. All anyone could hear were the sounds of machines and equipment clamoring and distressed voices talking over one another. It had been several minutes since Jennifer had stopped breathing so the medics decided to do an emergency cesarean to try and save the baby.

Within moments, they delivered a healthy eight pound five ounce baby boy from Jennifer's womb. Chaya and the children could hear the baby wailing from downstairs and for a moment they were relieved. Twenty more minutes went by before Dr. Overton came out of the bedroom towards Chaya and the children, looking flustered and exhausted.

"I'm so sorry, Chaya," he managed to say with a terribly somber look. "The baby is fine, but unfortunately, Jennifer didn't survive. They did all they could and if it wasn't for you, the baby wouldn't have made it either. I'm very sorry."

Chaya gasped in disbelief, and the children were inconsolable. The medics rushed the baby to the nearest hospital to give him a thorough check up as the others waited for the coroner to arrive. Rose had telephoned Teddy earlier, and he arrived in the middle of this horrific scene. He helped Chaya take the children out back so they wouldn't see Jennifer's body being carried out on the stretcher by the coroner to the awaiting transportation.

The autopsy revealed Jennifer died of a burst aneurism, a condition she apparently was born with, and there wasn't anything anyone could have done to prevent it. The added stress of the pregnancy placed too much strain on the vessel and it ruptured. The only comfort to Chaya and the children, was that the baby boy was born alive and apparently healthy, but their hearts were shattered and the thought of having lost Jennifer was just too much to bear.

30 | Coming Full Circle

"While we try to teach our children all about life,
our children teach us what life is all about."
~ Angela Schwindt

Chaya was given temporary custody of the baby until Jennifer's family could be notified. Two days later, Chaya brought home the baby boy Jennifer wanted to name Brian, Jr. The day was mixed with emotions as the joy of bringing a new baby home was overshadowed by the loss of Jennifer.

Jennifer had never discussed the exact details of where her family lived, but Chaya knew she had to find them and inform them of her passing and it was not something she was looking forward to. Chaya rummaged through Jennifer's purse looking for some kind of identification or information on her family, but there was nothing showing her family's address. As she opened and searched Jennifer's luggage, she found a vanilla cream linen envelope addressed to Jennifer in the inside lined pocket.

Chaya reached down to pick it up with her trembling hands and although she wanted desperately to open it, she felt she would be violating Jennifer's privacy, and decided to simply hold it and give it to her family once they were found. It was Teddy, with the help of a police detective, who located the family's address later that day who lived just a few hours away from the ranch.

After speaking with the detective, Chaya felt she should be the one to tell Jennifer's mother her daughter had passed, and deliver her new beautiful grandson to her. As she drove up the Alden driveway with Teddy and the baby in the car, with the detective in tow, she tried to find the words she would use to tell Jennifer's mother that her daughter had died, but she couldn't find any words that seemed appropriate.

"I can't do this, Teddy," she cried in anguish. "How do you tell someone that their child is dead? How do I do that?"

"It's not easy, Chaya, but trust in the Lord that you'll find the right words when you have to."

"She was such a beautiful person, Teddy."

"I know, honey. They don't make them better."

Standing at the doorway of Jennifer's family home with Brian Jr. all bundled up in her arms, Chaya turned around to look at grounds where Jennifer had grown up. The house was immaculately kept and the brush was trimmed in a perfect manner. The mailbox in front of the property was painted bright red, with the name Alden bolted on a black steel plate with shiny gold lettering. Four columns adorned the facade of this century-old two-story house which was surrounded by several acres of land. Chaya realized the tranquility of this peacefulness was about to be shattered with a few spoken words.

Chaya grabbed hold of the door knocker and gently hit it several times. "Hello, can I help you?" asked an elegant woman as she opened the door.

"Are you Mrs. Alden?" Chaya asked, almost hoping the woman would say "no, you have the wrong house."

"Yes I am. What can I do for you?"

"I knew your daughter, I mean I know your daughter, Jennifer, and this is Teddy, an old family friend of mine. May we please come in for a moment?"

"Oh my, you have a newborn with you. He's beautiful! Come on in, dear, where are my manners?"

"Thank you Mrs. Alden. He is beautiful, isn't he?"

Chaya handed the baby to Teddy, and asked Mrs. Alden to please sit down.

"Let me get you some tea first, then we'll all sit down to chat."

Chaya looked at Teddy hoping to receive a cue as to what to say next. Teddy just shrugged his shoulders and shook his head as he rocked the baby to soothe and quiet him down.

"So how do you know my Jen?" asked Mrs. Alden curiously.

"She came to my house about seven months ago."

"Oh yes, the Pastor told me Jen decided to visit a ranch and stay there a while. I only received one letter from her after she arrived at your home. I've been so worried, but I promised not to interrupt her retreat since I know she wanted some time to be alone."

"Mrs. Alden. There's no easy way to tell you this."

"Tell me what, my dear?"

"Jennifer. Jennifer was about to give birth to her child, and she... she... had a blood vessel burst in her head. She passed away, Mrs. Alden. You can't imagine how truly sorry I am. She was like family to me."

Katherine sat stoically in complete silence.

"Mrs. Alden, are you all right? What can I get for you?"

"What happened to the baby?" asked Katherine in a monotone tone.

"You have a beautiful grandson, Mrs. Alden. This is Brian, Jr., Jennifer's son," she said proudly as showed Mrs. Alden the baby.

Mrs. Alden just stared ahead without a sound. After what seemed like a long awkward moment, she asked if she could hold the baby. "May I ask what your name is?"

"Oh I'm so sorry, my name is Chaya. Chaya Rose. Your daughter had been staying at my ranch for the last seven months. She said she needed time to work out some things in her life and that she was pregnant. I told her she could stay as long as she wanted. I was so fond of your daughter Mrs. Alden. All the children were."

"How many children do you have?"

"Well, I have seven adopted children from mothers who couldn't take care of their babies for one reason or another. When Jennifer passed away, I went looking through her things to try to find a home address to notify you. Teddy here, found you with the help of a detective who's waiting outside. I have all her belongings in the car. I didn't know if this was the right time to bring everything to you, but I was sure you would like to have them."

"My dear, I don't think there will ever be a right time again."

"Mrs. Alden, I found this envelope in a side pocket of her suitcase, but it was still sealed." Chaya handed the closed envelope to Mrs. Alden and she took it in her hands, holding it in her lap with tears streaming down her face. Suddenly her face looked tired and old. Mrs. Alden caressed the envelope gently with her hand and handed it back to Chaya.

"She never opened it like I hoped she would. Miss Rose, this letter is for you now." Chaya starred at her completely bewildered.

"What do you mean Mrs. Alden? This envelope is addressed to Jennifer, and it says 'Important' on it. I really think you should read it."

"No my dear. You need to read it, because I know what it says. You see, I wrote it. When Jen told me she needed to go away to have some time to think, I believed what I wrote to her in this letter would help clear things up for her."

"I don't understand."

"You will my dear. Can we take a walk?"

Mrs. Alden took Chaya by her arm and led her to a beautiful area by the lake on her property. They sat in a gazebo style enclosure with angel ornaments surrounding a quaint limestone fountain.

"Chaya, please open the envelope and read the letter." Chaya obeyed, slowly opening the envelope, carefully as to not tear the flap too much as she pulled out a single, folded letter.

"Please read the letter out loud if you would."

"Are you sure Mrs. Alden?"

"Please. Go on and read the letter."

Chaya unfolded the letter, cleared her throat, and began to read.

Dear Jen,

As you learned before you left this morning, your father and I wanted to have a baby girl in addition to our three boys. I couldn't have any more children so we went to our church to see if there was anything they could do for us.

The Pastor there was a generous man with a lifelong mission to find homes for children whose parents were unable to take care of them. Well, it wasn't long before you came into our lives and I hope you know how much you were wanted not only by your father and I, but by your three brothers as well. We all adored you and you became your father's little girl the moment he laid his eyes on you.

I know you must be wondering why I'm telling you this now. Today you are leaving to think things out. I spoke with the Pastor yesterday, and he informed me of where he was sending you; a ranch where you could stay and hopefully decide to keep your baby.

My dear beautiful Jen, the Pastor told me yesterday that nineteen years ago, the lady who owns that ranch gave up a child herself. I don't know many of the details, but I do know that she had an impossible situation at the time with her own family, and she agreed to place her baby up for adoption like her father insisted.

It was a selfless act and she gave birth to a beautiful healthy baby girl she named Summer.

Chaya abruptly stopped reading and looked up towards Katherine. "How do you know all this?" asked Chaya, now with concern. "How could you possibly know all this?"

"Please continue with the letter dear."

"The Pastor informed me what the young lady named her baby, so when I brought you home, I wanted you to keep a part of her. That's why I named you, Jennifer Summer Alden. The name of the young lady who gave birth to you and allowed us to raise you as our own child is...Chaya Rose."

Chaya couldn't believe what she was reading and she gasped as the words started to sink in. That young girl who came into her life seven months ago was actually the daughter she placed for adoption some nineteen years ago.

"Chaya, are you all right?" asked Mrs. Alden in a worried tone. "Chaya, speak to me dear."

Chaya burst into tears holding both her hands to her mouth. She was still grieving the loss of her good friend and was unprepared to hear that the young girl who had been living with her and her children, was indeed her Summer Michael Rose.

"Oh my God!" Chaya blurted.

"That is your grandson, Chaya."

"Oh my God! It can't be!"

"It is dear. I'm so sorry you had to find out this way. When the Pastor told me where she was going, I had to let Jen know. I thought she had read the letter and stayed with you all this time, because she found out you were her birth mother."

Chaya was stunned and blankly stared at the floor in disbelief. "All this time, I had her so close to me."

"Chaya, at least you were able to get to know your daughter and spend time with her, and from what I can tell, you both cared very much for one another. That's more than a lot of people ever get."

Chaya stood up and struggled to steady herself, her legs shaking uncontrollably. She turned and walked back towards the house, where Teddy and the baby were waiting for her when he saw a look of despair on her face.

"Chaya, what's going on? Are you okay?"

"Teddy, he's my grandson. Brian is my grandson."

"What in the world are you talking about?"

"Jennifer was my daughter."

Teddy stood there with a shocked expression on his face. He knew Chaya placed a child for adoption many years ago, but nothing more was ever spoken about it.

"May the Lord have mercy!" he shouted out, shaking his head and staring at the ceiling.

"The Lord brought my daughter back to me, and now I've lost her again," Chaya uttered slowly. "I had her right there by my side all this time and I didn't even know it. All these years I prayed to have a chance to see and hold my little girl in my arms just once."

Chaya began to sob uncontrollably and Katherine rushed to her side, wrapping her arms around Chaya trying to comfort her.

"Chaya, I know how much pain you must be going through," Katherine said wiping away her own tears. "We've both lost our dear beautiful daughter, but the Lord also left us with a part of Jennifer you can hold onto."

"Yes he did, didn't he?" Chaya said as she looked over at Katherine. "And he gave me a chance to know my daughter and to finally hold her. My Summer."

As Katherine left the main room to get some tissues, Teddy walked over to where Chaya was sitting and handed her Brian Jr. When Mrs. Alden returned and walked into the main room, she stopped to look at Chaya, who was hugging the baby tightly.

Katherine clasped her arms to her chest said to herself, "The circle is now complete and there are no more secrets."

Chaya held the baby for a long while, as Katherine and Teddy stood by quietly when Katherine finally walked over to Chaya and sat down next to her.

"Chaya, I know you have your hands full with seven children, but if it's all right with you, would you be willing to raise Brian Jr.?" asked Katherine. "I live alone and I'm getting up in years now and I think it would be best if he grew up surrounded by a family who will take good care of him."

"I would be honored to," replied Chaya gazing into Brian's baby blue eyes.

31 | The Last Letter

"Some people come into our lives and quickly go.
Others stay for a while, leaving footprints on our heart
and we are never quite the same."
~ Author unknown

The children were excited when Chaya returned home with Brian Jr. after her visit with Katherine, since they weren't sure they would ever see the baby again. Chaya walked up to where all the children were gathered, handed Brian over to Rose, and asked her to watch him while she went outside. The children surrounded Rose to take a closer look at the baby while Chaya turned and walked out the front door, slowly heading toward the gardens to be by herself for a while.

Jennifer was laid to rest at the Alden family plot, next to her father. Chaya, Teddy and the entire family attended the funeral where they met Jennifer's three brothers. After Chaya and the family returned back home, she realized she had one more thing to do. That afternoon, Chaya drove to the lake where she and Michael said their marriage vows almost twenty years ago and where Summer was conceived. She wrote what would be her last letter to her daughter.

My dearest Summer,

I laid you to rest this morning, my sweet angel. It was the hardest thing I've ever had to do. You were and will always be the light of my life.

The Lord gave me a chance to know you, and for that, I'll be forever grateful. You were everything I thought you would be and more and I couldn't have asked for a better family to raise you.

I know now you were well taken care of and love surrounded your soul. That is a great comfort. You have left a tremendous void in my life and the children's, but you also gave them a piece of your spirit they will always take with them and that is to be treasured.

Summer, I now have the honor of raising your son, my grandson, Brian Jr. Although my heart is broken and heavy with sorrow, my heart also has room for even more love. I promise to take good care of your son, and through him, I will always have a part of you.

Sleep tight, my angel. Mommy will be with you one day again.

With all my love,

Your mother

32 | Epilogue
By Rose Summer Stuart

"A bird doesn't sing because it has an answer,
it sings because it has a song." ~ Maya Angelou

Momma raised Brian Jr. along with the rest of us. All the birth mothers continued to write letters to their children on Mother's Day and when the time was right, each child received a wooden box that Chaya had created for them that held the letters. It was always a moving experience to see each of my brothers and sisters read the letters and sometimes, the birth mother was there right by their side as they read them.

The Birth Mothers

"I have a lot of respect for my birth mother… I know she must
have had a lot of love for me to give me what she felt was a better
chance." ~ Faith Hill, Adoptee and Musician

Heather Stuart (Rose's birth mother): Although the Mother's Day letters arrived every year, Heather, my birth mother, decided it was best not to meet me unless I initiated the contact. She wanted my upbringing to be stable and knew Chaya was being a great mother to me and my siblings. When I turned twenty-two and was pregnant with the first of my four children, I sought out my birth mother, Heather.

We had an emotional meeting and were able to begin a relationship that lasts to this day. It was an amazing experience to have answers to all my questions, and although Heather is my birth mother and I am eternally grateful she gave birth to me, my adoptive mother Chaya has a huge part of my heart as the mother that gave me love every single day, held me, and brought me up to be the woman I am today.

Eve Woods (Alexander's birth mother): Eve chose to keep in touch with Chaya throughout the years and followed Alexander's life. She became an amazing woman, but her distrust for men was an obstacle that took years of therapy to overcome. After working full time at an abuse shelter, Eve went back to school and was able to go on to college with a scholarship she received. She became a certified counselor and continued her work at the women's abuse shelter. Eve's background gave her a unique perspective and personal understanding of the plight of these abused women and girls.

Ten years later, Eve married a good compassionate man named Shawn who she met in church. Shawn was a supportive husband who nurtured Eve and helped her overcome her fear of intimacy. They went on to have twin girls, Lucy and Lyla. When Alex turned eighteen, he received Eve's Mother's Day letters that she wrote every year, learning that Uncle Joe was his birth father and that he had two half-sisters. Alex meets with his sisters often and is thrilled to be in their lives.

Patricia Williams (Kendrick's birth mother): Patricia maintained a constant relationship with Kendrick throughout his life. She worked hard and studied to become a lawyer and even though Kendrick did not know Patricia was his birth mother until he was twelve at her request, she became a good friend to him and a mentor over the years. After he turned fifteen, they decided to give him the Mother's Day letters she had written to him throughout the years.

Kendrick always knew he was adopted, but was elated to find out his good 'friend' Pisha was really his birth mother. When he turned eighteen, Kendrick went out in search of his birth father and was able to track him down with Patricia's help. His father was a successful real estate contractor who bonded with his son instantly because of Kendrick's love of architecture.

Michael

"A first love always occupies a special place."
~ Lee Konitz

Michael, my mother's only romantic relationship in her life, married a schoolteacher several years after he graduated from college and had three beautiful children of his own. A year after Jennifer Alden (Summer Michael Rose) passed away giving birth to Brian Jr., Momma reached out to Michael to let him know he had been the birth father to Summer, and that she had passed leaving behind a grandson. It was one of the most difficult moments in her life, but my mother felt it was the right time and he deserved to know the truth. Needless to say Michael was stunned to learn of Summer existence, but understood my mother's situation at that time and her father's insistence to place the baby he never knew about for adoption. After twenty years, he came face to face with his first love, and his grandson, Brian Jr.

It was an emotional moment when they met and Michael gave Momma a warm embrace. Many tears were shed and when my mother introduced Brian Jr., and handed him his grandson to hold, Michael hugged him tightly and kissed his forehead over and over, shedding even more tears of both sadness and joy. Sadness that he never got the chance to meet his daughter, Summer, but joy that he would now be able to enjoy his grandson.

In the weeks that followed, Michael's wife met my mother and Brian Jr., and introduced their children to her and vice versa. Together, both of our families went to visit Summer's grave and placed roses on her tombstone. Although Momma only got to know Summer for seven months while she stayed at the ranch with us, she was able to provide Michael with more details about their daughter, her adoptive family the Aldens, and the baby's young father who passed, Brian Taylor.

Michael and his wife were involved throughout Brian Jr.'s upbringing and they became like family to my mother and all her children.

The Children

"There are only two lasting bequests we can hope to give our children. One of these is roots, the other, wings."
~ Johann Wolfgang von Goethe

As the years went by, I continued to assist Momma in her work helping other young mothers-to-be. Teddy, who passed away in 1969, left his entire estate to Momma. He lived such a modest life that no one had any idea his investments had grown to a substantial value and attached to his will, were letters he wrote to each of us. In 1970, with Teddy's endowment, our family officially opened The Chaya Rose Home for Girls, a safe home where pregnant young teens and women who have nowhere else to turn can come and live until they give birth.

Teddy was a treasure of a man and to this day, the letter he wrote to me is framed on the wall in The Chaya Rose Home for Girl's great room as a reminder of the selfless act of his love and generosity.

Momma lived long enough to see the birth of many of her grandchildren before she passed away peacefully in her late seventies. All her seven children and Brian Jr. were by her side as she took her last breath. At the funeral, the birth mothers came from all over the country to say their farewell to the woman who helped save them and their babies so many years ago.

Most of us are parents and grandparents now ourselves, and we've seen our family grow into an extended family of more than fifty and counting.

One thing that has kept us all bonded, is our love for our adoptive mother and her work and dedication to all her children. When we celebrated The Chaya Rose Home for Girls' 30th Anniversary in 2000, all my sisters and brothers were there to help with the expansion of a new wing.

Alex took time away from his successful landscaping business to plant and beautify the entire grounds surrounding the Home, taking extra care in designing more walkways and sitting areas to maximize and utilize the existing foliage. He was a master at it and his sons, who work with Alex in the family business, helped with the logistics and planning.

Kendrick, who achieved critical acclaim for his architectural achievements, designed and oversaw the construction of the new wing, making room for a library complete with computers and a study area, along with an educational learning section to upgrade the working skills of those staying at the Home. His design included a generous cafeteria-style kitchen with ample room to serve thirty at one sitting, and a large great room where the expectant mothers could sit, converse, relax or read, just like we had growing up. Kendrick also donated new wooden rocking chairs he built for the mothers to rock their newborn children in the maternity section of the Home.

Amanda, who became a successful interior designer, helped decorate and furnish the new wing with the generous donations from her colleagues at the interior design firm where she works at in New York City.

Jack and Jordon, retired from their professional football careers, were coaching at two different universities several states away. They were instrumental in raising funds at their schools and around the community to provide enough books, computers, desks, linen, and toiletries for the Home. Their tireless fundraising efforts were commendable and continue to provide for the Home to this day.

Sarah followed her caring nature and became a registered nurse, volunteering hundreds of hours at the Home, and providing much needed medical treatment. She resides in South Florida where she works at a healthcare facility and memorialized the only mother she ever knew with a brick in her honor at the Miami Cancer Institute's Meditation Garden.

Brian, Jr. turned out to be a great, compassionate man whose mission is helping the underprivileged. He founded a non-profit organization that helps feed the homeless and families in need throughout the state of Tennessee. Brian visits the Home often to volunteer his time and is currently writing a book about his experiences working with the underprivileged, donating all the proceeds to the Home.

As for me, I take great comfort knowing that the love and friendship Momma gave all of us, made a tremendous difference in her children's lives and in the lives of their birth mothers, and continues to do so. Although I miss her terribly, I take pride continuing to oversee The Chaya Rose Home for Girls knowing that Momma is smiling down on us from heaven. She not only opened her home to complete strangers in need, but she opened her heart as well. I will continue to see to it that her legacy is faithfully carried on. ~ Rose Summer Stuart

*This brick, on display at the Miami Cancer Institute's
Meditation Garden in South Florida, was donated to memorialize
and honor Chaya, the inspiration for this book
who passed away of a blood cancer.*